The Hypothesis of Giants

Book One: The Assumption

By

Melissa Kuch

ISBN:10 1479337358
ISBN 13: 9781479337354

Dedicated to my loving husband, Michael,
my third grade teacher, Lisa Dawber, and my father;
the first giant in my life who always told
me to reach for the stars.

If I have seen further than others, it is by standing upon the shoulders of giants.

—Isaac Newton

Contents

Chapter 1

Conch Shell

Nobody questioned the Sacred Hour in the town of Candlewick anymore. For the past fifteen years, everyone had learned to sleep through the bell chimes that rang out exactly one hour prior to the sun rising over the United States of the Common Good. The IDEAL, the leader of this newly founded country, enforced it strongly on the basis that it was to keep the people safe. There were rare occasions when an angry or defiant individual disobeyed this law. These unfortunate individuals were caught, imprisoned, and never heard from again. This Sacred Hour was deemed a symbol of unity among the people. This is the way it was and the way it would always be.

✵ ✵ ✵

It was a sweltering night in July, and the town of Candlewick was fast asleep during the Sacred Hour. But one girl awoke out of her slumber, eyelids open and ears perked up as if still in the confines of the dream. She froze, fearful that she had heard the sound in error and that she was imagining things. But then the deep bellowing noise echoed again from beyond her window sill. She sprang out of her bed and dashed to the opened window. She tried to discern from which direction the noise came. She held her breath, afraid that if she disturbed the silence of the night it would not sound again, counting the seconds in her head. Then it sounded again, loud and clear through the night, and the direction of its source was from the little ruby-red house directly opposite her on Wishbone Avenue.

No lights were on as the house lay hidden beneath the honey locust trees, with their long branches intertwined and thorns sticking upward like a spiked fence. The old weather-beaten shutters were hanging off their hinges as if they were fighting for survival, and the overgrown blades of grass resembled a wild prairie that had grown as high as the top of the front porch. A statue of a black cat stood guard beside the wicker rocking chair, and the paint was chipping off the scripted engraving of the number fifteen right above the chalky white screen door. The ominous street was vacant except for the occasional Common Good patrol car driving past, its headlights radiating through the shadows of the starless night, to ensure that curfew was being obeyed.

She heard the sound again. She could have sworn it was a conch shell resounding from the confines of the ruby-red house. It blew again, and she opened the window another inch and pressed her ear against the opening. It sounded like the musical outburst was searching the night for someone to hear its cry for help. Silence ensued again, and she whispered into the night, "I hear you. Do you need help? My name is Aurora."

The sound resonated again in her ears like a whisper in the night, translating itself inside her mind.

"Aurora."

Alarmed, she quickly slammed the window shut but fell backward over her tower of textbooks that were piled against the wall. She lay there, facing the ceiling and trying to catch her breath, her heartbeat racing. Then she dusted herself off and fixed her purple nightgown, covering her knees again before peeking through the cool glass of the window pane, resisting the urge to blink. Silence prevailed over the night as she waited for the conch shell to sound again. She stared into the darkness of the night but drifted off to sleep as the little ruby-red house stared back at her, unflinching.

✲ ✲ ✲

Fifteen-year-old Aurora Alvarez darted down the emerald carpeted stairs and entered the shambles that was the kitchen. She had wavy golden-brown hair that was cropped just above her shoulders, with a slight bang that was styled to the left side of her forehead. She rubbed the corner of her sunburnt cheeks that stood out over her naturally tanned complexion. She was about five foot six with wide, curvy hips and a nice sized bust that she held back against her chest with a sports bra. She possessed big, diamond-shaped brown eyes with thick eyelashes reminiscent of old Hollywood, a small, distinctive nose, and mauve lips that curled up to reveal a hint of two dimples when she smiled. Neighbors were keen on mentioning her beautiful features but her unfortunate weight. "The pretty frump girl," she was known as on Wishbone Avenue, as she had struggled with her weight since she was in elementary school. Though she was an active teenager, she did have a larger midsection than the other stick thin girls who attended Candlewick High School, which made her feel more like a giant compared to them.

Her parents were collectors of antique memorabilia and had run out of space in their house on Wishbone Avenue. They basically began piling knickknacks of all types of collections from baseball cards to Native American pottery to American Girl dolls in every open space they could find. It was like a discombobulated museum, and Aurora had to squeeze through the towering abyss to the kitchen table, where her father was hidden behind a pile of old history magazines; he made it a point to read at least one every morning before starting his day. She sat down in her chair, its metal legs screeching against the wooden floor.

"I heard it again last night, Dad."

Mr. Alvarez was immersed in his reading, and she watched him as his fingers kept getting stuck to the magazine pages as he tried to turn them. His cheek muscles twitched, knocking his reading glasses off the bridge of his sharp, pointed nose. He took a bite of whole grain toast, and bits of crumbs got stuck in his prematurely white mustache that contrasted with his chocolate-colored hair, combed ever so discreetly over his bald spot.

"Dad, I heard it again last night." Aurora repeated louder so that she was nearly screaming into his ear.

"What?" her father snapped back to reality. "Oh, it must have been the garbage truck making weird noises." He wiped the sweat from his brow and folded the magazine page over, the ink staining his fingertips.

"There was no garbage truck, Dad." Aurora folded her sleeves so that they were now like tank top straps over her shoulders. "Besides, it was at the Sacred Hour, and no garbage trucks come down our street at that time."

"You should be fast asleep at that hour," her father scolded, plopping the history magazine down in the read pile and picking up the next one sitting at the top of the unread pile. "You know fully well that no one is supposed to be awake and especially not go outside during the Sacred Hour. That mandatory curfew may be a power hungry mandate by the IDEAL, but this family is not ending up in Candlewick prison."

It reminded Aurora of the poem she had learned in her Kindergarten class:

Do not be found outside
During the Sacred Hour
The IDEAL has said it so
And the IDEAL has the Power.
When the sun awakens
You can awaken and should,
For the Awakened Hour
Is what's best for the Common Good.

Aurora bit her lower lip and asked, "Who in their right mind would want to get up at that hour anyway?"

Her father took his comb out of his breast pocket and tried to smooth what was left of his hair over his forehead. "It's been that way for the past fifteen years, right after you were born. It's the Common Good's way of imposing their laws on us. If they can control time, they can control anything."

He paused in mid stroke and then dropped the comb so that it collided onto the top of his history magazines pile. "No hablemos mas de eso. No more talk about that. Now name one of the battles won by General Washington during the Revolutionary War. You have five seconds. Go."

"Yorktown," she said with a yawn. "Don't you get tired of quizzing me on these history magazines?"

"It's important for us to remember our country's history, Aurora."

"They don't teach this stuff in school anymore. You know that. We have a new history."

Aurora took out the frying pan from beneath the sink and started mixing ingredients together in a bowl to make pancakes. She continued to look over her shoulder to make sure her father was too absorbed in his magazines to notice. She poured the gooey cream-colored batter into the pan and stood over them, eyeing the circular dots expanding and turning crispy brown on both sides. She flipped them over and her mouth started watering.

Her father wiped the crumbs off his mustache and continued, "Well, you'll be the smartest girl in the class when they decide to start teaching this again. Now, how did General Washington escape from the British after they were defeated in the Battle of Brooklyn? You have three seconds. Go."

"Snuck across the East River at midnight during a storm," Aurora spit out before her father could say, "Time is up." She laughed, sitting back down at the table, and poured maple syrup over her crispy brown pancakes. She took a big bite, savoring the taste of maple syrup drizzling down her throat, creating a sweet, sugary blend for her taste buds. She swallowed heartily and started to cut another piece, digging her fork into the fried doughy delicacy.

"Dad, did you not hear what I said before? The sound came from that creepy red house. I am sure of it. I could have sworn it was a conch shell. Remember when we heard them play it on that old video of *Lord of the Flies*? Anyway, you must have heard it. It was as loud and clear as anything."

"Did you know, Aurora, that in an ancient Hindu epic Mahabharata, the warriors of ancient India blew conch shells to announce battle?"

"Dad, are you listening to me?"

"Is she talking about Mrs. Taboo again?" Her mother's nightingale voice sounded behind a pile of comic books on the counter to the left of her. Her footsteps darted through the maze and headed straight for the coffee machine. Without her morning coffee, Mrs. Alvarez was a maniacal monster, so they kept a clear path for her to go to the coffee machine with no delay—the only clear path in the house. Aurora quickly shoved the rest of the pancake into her mouth to destroy the evidence before her mother could notice her through the box filled with the Captain America comic book series.

"She thought she heard music coming from their house this morning," her dad sighed, turning the page of his magazine and twirling his mustache with his other hand. "And at the Sacred Hour too."

"The Sacred Hour? That is three nights in a row. Aurora, this is not allowed, and you know it. Now stop with your stories and get dressed. You are going to be late for school."

"I know I heard it!" Aurora exclaimed, aggravated, and her chair screeched backward as she stood up and tiptoed her way toward her sanctuary, the bay window seat that faced Wishbone Avenue. She plopped herself down on the yellow cushioned seat and eyed the one-story ruby-red house directly across from their own. The curtains were still drawn, windows shut, and no air conditioner in sight. In this heat she was sure that whoever inhabited that house was either passed out or dead, their corpses decomposing while they ate their morning breakfast.

"It's too hot to shout, Aurora," she heard her mom's voice sound through the pile of carnival stuffed animals that made out the form of a doorway between her living room and kitchen. She heard her slurp down the black substance as if she was consuming the elixir of life. "Rumor has it that our neighbor Old Mr. Harold saw Mrs. Taboo."

"When was this?" Her dad's ears perked up, and the history magazine slid down onto his lap. "When were you going to tell me?"

"I didn't know you cared," Mrs. Alvarez laughed, taking a long slurp. "I mean it's been about three months since she went away on vacation. She apparently told Old Mr. Harold that she was away visiting grandkids, but she'd never spoken about them before. What grandmother isn't raving about her grandkids? Honestly. And her black hair was streaked with white highlights. I should give her the name of my hairdresser. She's really the best Candlewick has to offer. Anyway, while he was speaking to her, a delivery man came up with a mysterious package."

"Why mysterious?"

"Because Old Mr. Harold swears it was not Rick, our usual mailman. This delivery man wasn't wearing a mailman uniform or driving a mail truck. Mrs. Taboo turned white as a ghost when she received this package, and once the delivery man had driven away, she hastily told Old Mr. Harold she had to leave and slammed the door swiftly behind her. Can you believe that?"

"She probably was in a hurry." Her father huffed and returned to his reading.

"But this was over a week ago, and Old Mr. Harold hasn't seen her leave that house since. And I haven't seen her. I have been looking at her rundown house, and the blinds are still drawn."

Mr. Alvarez slammed the magazine down on top of the table. "Is Inspector Herald now forcing us to spy on our neighbors? That was McCarthyism and the Salem witch hunt, or have people forgotten that?"

"Charles, we may not like everything about the Common Good government, but it is better than what we had. Remember when there were those horrible religions fighting against each other? We needed the IDEAL to step in and contain those fanatics and make peace at whatever cost was necessary. Remember, what is best for the common good is what's best for everyone. Now stop reading those magazines and get ready for work. Candlewick Courthouse needs their finest attorney."

"Listening to you is like listening to all that blasted propaganda back at the office."

Aurora had ceased listening to her parents bicker and instead contemplated Mrs. Taboo. She was curious to find out if Mrs. Taboo was the one who'd been playing the conch shell during the Sacred Hour. And if so, why was Aurora the only one who heard it? Just then her mother's voice made her stomach churn.

"Who made the pancakes?"

Aurora quickly licked a smidgen of syrup off her lips and replied hastily, "What pancakes?"

"Charles! I told you she is on a strict diet. Her doctor gave us strict instructions."

"I didn't even realize she was eating pancakes. Now, Aurora, what did Benedict Arnold do that caused him to become a traitor? You have five seconds."

Her mother yanked the magazine out of his hands, tearing a sliver of the page. "Do you want your daughter to be overweight forever? I mean, she is fifteen years old! These are crucial years."

"I think she looks fine," her father said, pulling the magazine back. "Now look what you did. Where is the glue?"

"Charles, she is bigger than all the other girls on Wishbone Avenue. We have to support her. And if I could survive on a soup diet—where I lost ten pounds, mind you—then Aurora can survive with grapefruits. Aurora, do you hear me? Now if I catch you with pancakes again I will take away your TV privileges for a month. So go to your room and get dressed. You have school. And don't forget the block party is this Saturday."

"I'm not going," Aurora cried out, fixing her nightgown that was riding up her legs. "I'm not going, and you're not going to make me!"

"I bought you that nice indigo dress. I put it in your closet upstairs."

Aurora felt her temperature rising as her mind swirled in circles. "It was for a size 12. I am a size 14, Mom!"

"Well, you are going to fit into a 12. No daughter of mine is wearing a size 14 dress."

Aurora stumbled over the empty cereal boxes and stormed up the stairs until she was back in her room. She slammed the door shut, rattling the pictures of the Mayan ruins and the pyramids of Egypt that were fastened to her silver walls. She straightened the picture of the rainbow over the Great Wall of China, closed her eyes, and imagined climbing up the steps, admiring the view at the top, and having a picture of her taken on that iconic masterpiece of mankind.

She circled her room and grimaced at the pictures that someone else had taken. Not her.

"One of these days I will be the one going on the adventure, not just reading about it. I am going to live it."

The crooked picture of the glaciers in the Arctic Circle swayed back and forth like a hypnotic pendulum as she yanked her school uniform off the hanger and put it on.

Chapter 2

School Drama

Aurora sat on the curb in front of the corner stop sign where Wishbone Avenue ran perpendicular to Main Street. She felt like she wanted to tear her school uniform off her sweltering body. The white cotton blouse was sticking to her chest, and the indigo skirt that stopped right below her kneecap was sticking to her legs like adhesive tape. And of course the outfit was not complete without the orange socks that she had rolled down over the front loop of her black dress shoes. She tossed her thick wavy hair back into a ponytail, despite her mother's protests that she looked too much like a tomboy with her hair up.

She sat looking down Wishbone Avenue, the curvy, zigzagging street that she'd lived on her whole life with hardly anything ever changing. She eyed the different styled houses that nearly matched the personalities of their inhabitants. There was the house of Hattie Pearlton, the most popular girl in their sophomore class, with the perfectly manicured lawn, Romanesque fountain, and beautiful, outlandish hydrangea bushes encircling the large nauseating structure of a mustard yellow country house. Then there was the large purple Victorian house of her science teacher Mrs. Xiomy, who lived in the cul-de-sac at the end of Wishbone Avenue. And of course there was the house of Jonathan and Boreas Stockington, who lived in what she called the Stockington mansion. It was a large brick colonial-style house with three chimneys and an acre and a half of land, which had both a tennis court and pool in the backyard. She always wondered which room belonged to Jonathan. She walked past this house every day going to school, hoping to catch a glimpse of him walking on the opposite side of the street so she could maybe gather up enough nerve to wave at him. And maybe he would wave at her or catch her eye and smile that perfect smile that made her heart flutter.

All of a sudden she was whisked in the head with a flying scrunchie.

Aurora opened her eyes with a start to behold her friend Mary Fray nearly tackling her on the corner.

"Mary, that could have hit me in the eye."

Mary threw her backpack down onto the ground and stretched up toward the sky, letting out a huge yawn. "Just checking to make sure you were alive. You looked like you were daydreaming in broad daylight. The Inspector might make that illegal. You don't want to get sent away to Candlewick Prison, do ya? "

Mary's thick blonde eyebrows furrowed over her pointy nose and contrasted with her dyed black hair. Her overgrown bangs nearly covered her big owl eyes. A rose tattoo etched into her skin on the top left shoulder blade. She refused to wear the entire school uniform, always managing to find a way to add a touch of her personality into the structured outfit mandated by the school board. Today it was mismatched socks, the required orange sock on her left leg and a knee-length red-and-white polka dot sock on her right.

Aurora laughed as her friend tried to blow a bubble with some bubblegum she'd probably stolen from Ernie Levitz, a freshman who'd had a crush on Mary since the first grade.

"First of all, you only get arrested if you get caught outside at the Sacred Hour, like Boreas Stockington. That's why he ended up in prison."

"Yeah, well, he has always been begging for attention." Mary chewed and chewed. They started walking down Main Street toward Candlewick High School. While Mary was trying to keep up with her friend's long strides, she said, "I wonder how Boreas did it."

Aurora shrugged, wiping a bead of sweat that was dripping down her forehead. "Did what?"

"How he got out of Candlewick Prison alive, silly. I wish he would tell someone already."

Aurora shrugged and then froze as she looked up. On the opposite side of the street was none other than Hattie Pearlton walking arm in arm with Jonathan Stockington. Jonathan stood tall with his long honey-blond hair pulled back in a ponytail, his uniform pressed and perfectly tailored over his physique. He had bright turquoise eyes, high cheekbones, and a silver stud earring in his left ear. His hand was latched onto Hattie's, and she was standing beside him like she had won the lottery. Her perfect hair cascaded down her back, and she wore a white tank top; her uniform skirt hiked up over the knee so it accentuated her slender legs. She was encircled by a group of the popular students, who were gossiping and every now and then turning in Aurora's direction, pointing and laughing. Aurora looked away then turned her back on them because just thinking about what they were saying was enough to make her nauseous. She was glad Mary was walking with her. She always felt safer with Mary around.

Mary blew another big pink bubble that exploded, causing little bits of bubblegum to get stuck across her lips and cheeks.

"I wonder what Jonathan Stockington sees in that dimwitted Barbie doll."

Aurora blushed at the mere mention of Jonathan's name. Aurora had had a crush on Jonathan Stockington since the third grade. He was highly renowned at their school, being captain of the high school football, baseball and basketball teams. He was student body president and even was the lead in the high school musical *Anything Goes*. Aurora, who couldn't sing or dance for the life of her, actually tried out for the play in the hopes of getting a chance to be close to him. Of course she didn't make it after making a fool of herself attempting to do the Charleston dance routine and falling flat on her butt in front of the entire theater club.

"I think I have given up on him ever knowing I'm alive."

Mary pushed her friend playfully. "Please. You can do so much better than a Stockington. You know that boy Harold Horsegraves has been itching to ask you out."

Aurora made a gagging expression, and they laughed as they picked up the pace, realizing they were running late. Main Street consisted of cobblestone sidewalks with lamp posts on each corner. They passed the Candlewick Library, a big colonial-style brick building with high security surrounding its perimeter since it was only to be utilized by the Common Good officials. The public was not permitted to enter the grounds, but Aurora couldn't help but wonder what they were hiding within their walls.

They passed little Fanny Sue's Bakeshop, which smelled of cupcakes and croissants, and the scent made their stomachs wish to linger a moment or two longer. They ran passed the beautiful thirty-story white marble Candlewick Government building where Inspector Herald and his Common Good officials were stationed. It was the most modern edifice in the entire county since it had been rebuilt after it had nearly burned to the ground ten years earlier. The flag was already raised at half-staff in honor of the Independence Day of the Last Straw, which would be celebrated that weekend. The orange flag featured an indigo stitch outline of the country with **THE IDEAL** spelled out in bold letters in the dead center of the flag.

Aurora paused for a minute to look at the government building. Her father worked somewhere on the fifth floor, but she was always prohibited from visiting. Inspector Herald, worked in the office at the very top of the building, the penthouse, overlooking all of Candlewick and the Atlantic Ocean. It was the only office that had a circular balcony surrounding it and if Aurora strained her eyes she could make out the outline of the telescope that, rumor had it, was used by the Inspector to gaze down onto the graveyard of those who had fallen in the Last Straw Protest.

The Last Straw Protest was fifteen years earlier when the religious protestors had one final stand against the IDEAL and the Common Good government. It resulted in a massacre, with many innocent people killed, and caused the collapse of the protests across the country. With no one else to interfere, the IDEAL, along with Inspector Herald and the Common Good Party, were able to rise to power; the right to freedom of speech and religion were abolished for the greater cause. The IDEAL said that if everyone conformed to one idea, then there would be no fights or wars over opposing thoughts or beliefs. No one ever saw the IDEAL. Inspector Herald from Candlewick was his second in command, ensuring that the country followed the IDEAL's rules and teachings or paid the consequences.

Aurora gazed through the thick barbed wire fence to behold the line of gravestones that were barely visible from view. Aurora's father had told her that even IMAM, the leader of the religious rebellion, was buried there. He had been the one who had organized the Last Straw Protest, and he was executed by the Inspector himself for his crimes of conspiring against the country. It was rumored that the Inspector liked to keep the rebel's gravestone there as a reminder that it was he who had crushed the leader of the rebellion all those years before and that he would not hesitate to stop anyone else who tried to rise up against him.

Aurora took a peek through the fence to catch a glimpse of the infamous leader's grave, a game a lot of the other students played when they were younger. She thought she saw a glimpse of the pink marble stone and of a woman planting a forever flower at the grave site. The woman was wearing a dark cape over her body, but a few blonde strands were whisked out from beneath the hood. She looked to be digging. Aurora tried to get a better look, but then Mary's voice called out, "Come on, Aurora, you slowpoke. We're going to be late."

When Aurora turned back, the woman had vanished. A cool, brisk wind crawled over her skin, and immediately Aurora ran away from the government building. Adjacent to that building was the Candlewick Prison, and she did not want to linger too long and become a permanent resident.

They were about a block and a half away from the school when Aurora shuddered at the sight of Joshua's Laundromat boarded up with a sign "For Rent" blasted on the front in red paint. There was graffiti over the entire store with illegible symbols that Aurora had never seen before.

"I can't believe Joshua's Laundromat is out of business. We've been coming here as long as I can remember," she said nostalgically.

Mary took her red lipstick out of her purse, knelt down, and made a mark on the door of what resembled a star, but more like two triangles superimposed.

"What are you doing?" Aurora cried out, trying to cover her friend from sight.

"Joshua was my family's friend. This is a symbol for our people."

Aurora took her friend's hand and yanked her to her feet. "Mary, I don't know what has gotten into you, but you could get into loads of trouble for drawing things like that. What if someone saw you?"

"So what? I am so sick and tired of everyone looking away when something like this happens."

Aurora stared at her friend in disbelief. "Something like what? The store went out of business. It happens."

"That's not what I'm talking about." Mary leaned in close, her eyes looking troubled as she whispered, "I'm talking about the disappearances."

Aurora felt her body go numb as she stared again at the boarded up store, and her mind started racing about the others on their street that had suddenly vanished out of nowhere. The local grocer Mr. Lee, the fisherman Benny Breezeworthy, and even the Mulberrys. They had all moved without a word. The newspaper had a story for them all, but they were never seen or heard from again. Mary was right. There were many disappearances that nobody questioned. The only one who had returned after disappearing was Boreas Stockington.

Her thoughts were interrupted by the sound of the school bell, and both Mary and Aurora dashed as fast as they could toward the school building to make it to their first class, which was science. Their teacher, Mrs. Xiomy, would not be happy they were late.

✲ ✲ ✲

Mrs. Xiomy silenced the class with a loud chemistry explosion that shook the entire classroom and caused a hole in the ceiling. The whole front row was whisked back and nearly thrown from their chairs. Mrs. Xiomy removed her goggles, and her bright blonde hair stuck straight up from the aftermath of the explosion.

"Good morning, class," she said in her high soprano voice with a slight Middle Eastern accent. Though eccentric at times, she was one of the better teachers at the school. "That's what we call another example of Newton's Third Law of Motion. For every reaction there is an equal and opposite reaction. Can anyone explain what caused that explosion?"

She pointed at Hattie Pearlton, who stood there befuddled from the explosion with a spilled bottle of Diet Coke on her desk. "You're trying to kill me!" she shrieked, trying to get some of the soda off her tank top. "This will never come out!"

"That will teach you to wear your school uniform to class, Miss Pearlton. Anyone else?"

Aurora's hand shot up and once called upon said, "You created a chemical reaction mixing the Alka-Seltzer tablets and water. This chemical reaction causes the massive buildup of pressure. Eventually the gas pressure needs to be released, so the rocket is pushed upward out of the film canister as the gases are exhausted downward. Now the rocket is lodged in the ceiling or maybe somewhere in Mr. Smith's math class."

Mrs. Xiomy amethyst eyes gleamed. "That is correct." She turned to the blackboard and started writing, and Mary patted Aurora on the back.

Just then the classroom door shot open, and in walked Principal Borscht, a short, rotund man who resembled an oompa loompa, followed by Boreas Stockington. Boreas was marched to the front of the classroom, his thick black hair gelled up and his school uniform on backward. Boreas was also a sophomore at Candlewick High but barely attended class and, unlike his brother Jonathan, was considered a failure by most teachers and students. Boreas was the polar opposite of his family lineage; where his father and brother strove for perfection, Boreas did not. Except for tennis. He had agreed to join the team, and to everyone's shock he was really good. Aurora had actually watched some of the games when she was hiding from Hattie Pearlton's wrath behind the football bleachers after school. Boreas was the best player on the team, with a serve of seventy miles an hour that crushed his opponents. His broad shoulders, defined arms, and six-feet-tall stature also helped his game. She remembered hearing some of the students in class say they actually had a chance to make postseason this year. Many girls thought he was cute, except for the scowl plastered on his face.

Principal Borscht fixed his dress shirt collar, his face plum-red, and said in his thick Russian accent, "Now think about what I said, Boreas. This is the first time in ten years we could make the playoffs, and your ego is not going to take this away from me or this school. You have twenty-four hours to think this over, or else I have no qualms with putting you in detention for the rest of the school year."

The entire class erupted in disbelief over Boreas's act of betrayal to the school, and even Aurora turned to Mary in shock, but she was busy scribbling on a piece of loose-leaf paper.

The Principal went up to Mrs. Xiomy and whispered something in her ear. Mrs. Xiomy's face went pale, and she said softly, "Please excuse me for five minutes. I will be right back. And no touching the chemicals while I am away or there will be hell to pay when I return."

The door shut behind them, and instantly Hattie stood up and moved her hands like she was parting the sea and strutted toward Aurora with an evil twinkle in her eye. Before Aurora even had time to react, Hattie had swooped down and knocked the binder off her desk; it crashed onto the floor, her notes scattered under her desk.

"That's what you get for making me look bad in front of Mrs. Xiomy."

Aurora felt the whole classroom staring at her, and she sputtered, "I don't know what you are talking about, Hattie." She slowly knelt down to pick up the papers but was self-conscious, as if her pants were going to split down the seam.

"You know exactly what you did," Hattie bellowed in her nasal voice. "You had to show off in front of the whole class and describe the explosion in perfect detail when you know perfectly well I had no idea what she was talking about."

"So you just looked bad on your own," Mary chimed in, now standing up. Though a mere height five foot one, she held her head up high, and for a second Hattie looked inferior.

"Stay out of this, Fray," Hattie exclaimed, regaining her composure once she realized her posse was still backing her. "I don't know why you hang out with Fatty Alvarez anyway."

Mary was still chewing her gum, and before anyone had a second to blink, she spit the gum out of her mouth. Hattie ducked at the last minute, and the huge wad of gum ended up going into the hair of Boreas Stockington. Mary and Aurora both held their breath as he pulled the sticky substance out of his hair, crumbled it up into a ball, and held it in his fist as if he were ready to strike.

Instead of throwing it at Mary, he stuck it aggressively under Mrs. Xiomy's desk, followed by a thunderous applause from the cronies. He wiped his hand on the side of his jeans and then sat on the edge of the desk, staring so intently at Aurora that she felt stupid as she continued putting the papers back on her desk and trying to get them organized into their proper order.

Hattie let out a giant humph and retreated back over to her circle of friends.

Aghast, Aurora turned to Mary and whispered, "I can't believe you stood up for me in front of Hattie. I don't know what to say."

Mary smiled. "You would have done the same thing for me."

Aurora resumed putting the sheets of paper back into her binder, feeling like a coward and wondering if she would have hid under the desk instead of standing up for her friend. She clicked the binder clips shut and put her face in her hands.

Hattie marched over to Boreas and demanded, "Where the hell were you this morning? Jonathan wants to talk to you."

Boreas put his legs on his desk and laughed outright. "I'm sure he does, along with the rest of the tennis team, my coach, my dad, and probably the whole damn school."

Another boy named Henry, who was on the tennis team, cried out, "You'd better not quit the team, Boreas. If I were you I'd march back into the principal's office and say you changed your mind."

Henry pushed Boreas, who took it without any resistance. Aurora thought there was going to be another fight, and Mrs. Xiomy was nowhere to be found.

"Look, I quit the tennis team. It's my business why I did, so just leave me alone."

"Do you think about anyone but yourself? We're talking about making the *playoffs!*"

Boreas slammed his fist against the desk. "It's not my fault all of you suck."

Henry pushed the desk out of the way, the legs screeching against the floor like chalk on the blackboard, and Boreas stood up as if waiting for the punch. Henry looked bewildered, not expecting Boreas to actually fight, but then before he could make a fist the door flew open and five Common Good officials marched into the room. Everyone jumped back into their seats like robots as the officials filed in, their metallic badges glistening on the right side of their uniforms. The slogan *The IDEAL for Unity* was embroidered alongside their sleeve. They marched in unison down the aisle, their shadows engulfing the light in the room, and their footsteps sounded like drums beating mercilessly in mechanical rhythm. Nobody dared take a breath as their shadows passed their desks. They stopped marching right in front of Mary's desk. The front guard spoke in a monotone voice, "Mary Fray, we need to take you in to headquarters for questioning."

Mary stood up, not flinching or looking fazed by this spectacle happening in the first period science class.

"What did she do?" Boreas cried out, getting to his feet again, but he was immediately knocked down by another guard. Aurora stood stark still and watched the scene playing out as if it was a bad dream. But the scene continued, and Mary packed up her bag, looked at Aurora with courage in her eyes, and mouthed, "I'll be okay." She then was marched out of the classroom, the door slamming shut behind them.

Aurora snapped out of her momentary stupor, jumped out of her seat and ran to the classroom door. She grabbed the handle, prepared to run after Mary and force them to let her friend go, when someone held her back. She screamed at the top of her lungs. She had to help her. She had to save her. She screamed as loud as she could, but Mary was gone.

Chapter 3

The Block Party

The thermometer read 105 degrees, and it was by far the hottest day of the summer. Children were bursting open fire hydrants to soak in the cool, crisp water as the sun streamed down on them from above, its golden ball gloating and piercing their skin with its ever-present rays. Old Mr. Harold was rocking on the front porch of his house painted in honor of the Independence Day of the Last Straw. The colors of orange and indigo adorned the walls of his duck-shaped house, whilst the day before it had been painted the shade of red. No one on Wishbone Avenue knew how he was capable of painting the house so quickly, especially at his age. He now was looking content and fanning himself with a decorated fan with the words "The IDEAL has Spoken" sketched over the parchment in black scripted ink. He was awaiting the parade that would begin exactly at an hour past the Awakened

Hour. Everyone on Wishbone Avenue would soon join him on their front porches, fans held high in hand, as the hour was approaching. The heat couldn't jeopardize the parade since the IDEAL declared it so. And everyone wanted to emulate the IDEAL. Old Mr. Harold gazed at his next door neighbor's house, which was a white two-story house with red shutters. He thought the Alvarez household just needed a shade of blue to start a controversy in the town, as red, white and blue were the old and forbidden colors of the United States of America. He wondered why his neighbors weren't out of their house yet. He was rocking back and forth on his patio swing, contemplating giving them a call to make sure that they remembered what day it was. But of course everyone remembered what day it was.

The indigo dress was too tight, as Aurora had predicted, yet her mother was resolute on making her fit into the garment. She forced her daughter to suck in all the air she could muster in order to zip it up. It clung to her body like a corset, and Aurora feared if she sat down the entire dress would rip in two. She had not gotten much sleep the night before, having heard the conch shell sound again during the Sacred Hour. She thought it best to not tell her parents. They would most likely have the same reaction, and she didn't want to end up in the Candlewick loony bin since once again she appeared to be the only one who had heard it.

Her mother pranced out in a dandelion-patterned sundress that hugged her shapely hips and backside and a large white brimmed beach bonnet that was tilted ever so slightly to the side over her ebony curls. Aurora followed suit with her own orange bonnet set on top of her thick wavy hair that was sticking to the back of her neck. She wanted to tie it up in a ponytail, but her mother insisted that it be kept down.

"Don't you want to represent the Alvarez family beauty? You look so much better with your hair down. Everyone always says that. They say, 'Norma, your daughter looks like a goddess with her hair down.'"

"Yeah," Aurora thought. "Then they would add 'Frump Girl' to the end of the sentence."

Mother and daughter Alvarez stood out like sore thumbs dressed for a garden party, as the rest of the neighbors were dressed in shorts and t-shirts for the barbecue festivities. Everything was decorated with indigo and orange, from balloons, to tablecloths to even the flags hanging from each of the houses on Wishbone Avenue.

Old Mr. Harold stood up from his porch swing and bowed to the two women as they passed him. "I was afraid you would both miss the parade this morning."

"Never, Mr. Harold." Aurora's mother smiled her obsequious grin as if she was meant for politics. "And what a beautiful parade it was. The children looked so adorable marching this morning. I remember when my Aurora used to be in the parade."

"You couldn't miss Aurora." Mr. Harold laughed until he hiccupped. "Is Mr. Alvarez down by the barbeque?"

"He is down at the courthouse on Inspector Herald's orders. Apparently there is a case of the utmost importance to discuss, even on holiday. He'll come around later this afternoon."

Mrs. Alvarez smiled her gallant white smile at her neighbor and sauntered past as Aurora struggled to keep up. Mrs. Alvarez sidestepped to her friends Rose Champagne and Gabrielle Wilson, who were sitting down in lounge chairs on the street, sipping sangria cocktails. Her mother put on her designer sunglasses (another thing she collected, having 500 pairs in different sizes and styles), and found a place beside the other women to sunbathe.

"I am sweating bullets," Gabrielle stated frankly. She was a pretty black woman with dyed platinum blonde hair that she had tied back with a clip. "I should have told Theo yes when he asked if I wanted to go on that Alaskan cruise for this holiday."

"But then you would have missed out on this fun-filled weekend," Rose retorted while fixing her hair, the color of her name. Though only forty years old, she regularly received Botox injections, and her face was as tight as the dress on Aurora's body. It looked as if by a simple touch her face would break into a million pieces. Her breasts were also a size double-D and were popping out of her bathing suit so that every man who passed by couldn't help but stare in that direction. Aurora recalled that one night her parents and Rose had gone out to dinner and when they returned home, her mom slapped her father, saying the entire time he was gazing at Rose's assets. Her father had retorted that it wasn't his fault Rose's assets were more refined than what came out of her mouth.

"How is husband number three?" Mrs. Alvarez asked, applying sunscreen to her skin.

"Charles is working with Henry Stockington on the barbeque in the back. You know Henry and his perfectly grilled hamburgers. I think my husband is trying to learn his secret. Henry's boy Jonathan has grown into such a good-looking young man. Oh, to be a teenager again."

Gabrielle nodded. "Jonathan is such a handsome boy. And his younger brother Boreas I swear is the spitting image of his mother. It's like staring at a ghost each time I see him. Such a shame those poor boys lost their mother so young. What is it now? Ten years ago? It's not right that Henry never remarried and those boys grew up without a mother. Oh, Aurora, I didn't see you there. Come sit down beside us."

"No, thank you. I'd rather stand," Aurora said flatly, afraid that her dress would rip and then if Hattie Pearlton found out, the entire high school would know by dinnertime.

"What a pretty dress," Gabrielle said, removing her sunglasses so that they sat on the tip of her nose as she eyed her up and down. "I say, the girls are wearing dresses tighter than we used to back when we were young girls."

"I think Aurora might pop out," Rose giggled under her breath, taking another sip of the cocktail.

"Be careful, Norma. The boys on this block might be paying your little girl a little too much attention. She has some nice womanly curves that could get the boys a bit too excited."

Mrs. Alvarez chugged her glass of sangria. "Ladies, that's no way to talk. She's only fifteen years old."

"As if you don't remember what it was like to be fifteen years old with the captain of the football team chasing you behind the bleachers," Gabrielle snorted, playfully tapping Mrs. Alvarez on the back.

"Believe me when I say I was a different woman than my Aurora. We can both say as much."

"But the boys haven't changed much over the years."

They continued to reminisce about the old days, and Aurora found her opportunity to slip away unnoticed. The block was a whirlwind of excitement and pretty much everyone was outside sitting on folding chairs. Food was set up on long tables in front of everyone's house, inviting people from their block to partake and enjoy. The scent of roasting meat and corn on the cob resonated in the air, and though extremely hungry she only took a piece of watermelon and continued along her exploration. A few neighbors nodded at her and asked whether her mother was there. She nodded in between bites and spit out a few black seeds, which spun out of her mouth like bullets. She watched as other girls and boys from her grade met like herds on the street corners or in the pool, wondering what it would be like if she was popular like Hattie Pearlton. She continued sucking at the juice of her watermelon as her mind was in a dreamlike state picturing herself as Hattie Pearlton with handsome Jonathan Stockington.

Old Mr. Harold snapped Aurora out of her daydream by calling out her name in a high falsetto voice and waving his arms like a madman from his front porch.

"Hey, Aurora, can you get me a hamburger like a good girl? And no cheese. I hate cheese. And maybe a pickle if they have one. And onions. I love onions."

"Sure, Mr. Harold," she said nonchalantly. Then she bit her lip, looking around to make sure no one else was within earshot, and added, "Have you heard of any news about Mary Fray and her family?"

Mr. Harold tickled a bit of gray stubble under his chin and said, "I believe the newspaper said they moved to Iowa. That's what I read. They were bankrupt and had to move in a hurry because her father found a job out there on a farm."

Aurora tried to smile as she threw the stump of her watermelon into the garbage, clanging against the side. That was the same story she had heard for the past week, and none of it made any sense. She had run to Mary's house after school that day, and it was completely empty as if it has been uninhabited for weeks. The only thing she still had was the piece of loose leaf paper that Mary had been scribbling on in class before the Common Good officials took her away. It was that funny star that she had drawn on the closed down Laundromat earlier that same morning, the two inverted triangles. Aurora hoped her friend was all right, but how would she find her in Iowa—if she was even there?

Aurora maneuvered her way through the crowds to the checkered patterned tablecloth that housed the hamburgers still sizzling from being recently charbroiled. The Stockington spread was always the best every year with hamburgers, hot dogs, filet mignon, and the best hot wings in the town. She stood waiting on the line that wrapped around with the end near the Stockington backyard. There were at least thirty people in front of her, and she leaned against the chimney, resting her head against the brick stones.

"I told you I don't care about this stupid barbeque," a voice sounded from behind the house.

The line started moving forward, but Aurora ignored it and peered out from behind the chimney toward the drama ensuing in the backyard of the Stockington mansion.

"I ask you to do one thing for me. Watch the hamburgers. And you burn them. Can you not do anything right?"

Aurora spotted Henry Stockington, who was a tall white man in his early forties with bright blonde hair and thick eyebrows. His veins were bulging out of his high forehead and he was busy scolding his son Boreas, whose head was pointed downward, his hands fidgeting. Boreas was wearing a navy blue shirt and khaki shorts, and his thick black hair was disheveled and spiked up over his forehead, with one strand out of place and falling over his distinctive oval eyes. Boreas had his mother's Asian features and darker undertones, as opposed to Jonathan, who took after his father's lighter European heritage.

"Why can't you be more like your brother?" Mr. Stockington screamed, again his vein in his forehead throbbing. "He would never have burned these hamburgers. I can't trust you with one simple task!"

"I told you I didn't mean to burn them," Boreas exclaimed, glaring back at his father with great animosity. He looked as if he would stand his ground, but then he backed down. It was a fleeting moment of a courageous act, but it was quickly forgotten. "I know that this is about the tennis championship."

"I told you I don't want to talk about that, especially not here."

"Can you let me explain—"

"I have had the principal and everyone in your school calling me about how you have failed them, and you know what I said? I told them I am not surprised. Not surprised that you let them down because you have never once been anything but a failure in my household."

Boreas opened his mouth to say something but then immediately shut it. His father grabbed the spatula and started flipping new burgers onto the grill.

"You're done for the day. Get out of my sight."

"Whatever! I didn't even want to be here. You and Jonathan can be one big demented happy family!"

Boreas started to storm away when Mr. Stockington grabbed him roughly by the arm and whirled him around to face him. He then looked up with his thick framed glasses and caught Aurora staring at them from behind the chimney. She shrunk back, wishing she could disappear as she felt his eyes digging into her own.

"Did you want something?" he shouted.

"Old Mr. Harold asked me to get him a burger."

"Well, then go get one."

Boreas turned to face her, and his eyes penetrated into her own with such loathing that she felt her entire body go cold with his resentment. She immediately made a 180-degree turn and scampered off toward the hamburger line, cursing at herself under her breath for letting her curiosity once again get the best of her. Why couldn't she have just gotten the burger like she was supposed to and not go deviating from her mission?

She grabbed the first burger on top and plopped it down on a paper plate and grabbed a handful of pickles sprinkling them around the burger, but then couldn't remember if Old Mr. Harold wanted pickles or onions. Or both. While deliberating this information and knowing fully well Old Mr. Harold would hate anything she brought back to him, she ran smack into Hattie Pearlton whose arm was linked with none other than Jonathan Stockington.

"Well if it isn't Fatty Alvarez," Hattie snorted. Her all-too-perfect blue jeans hugged her size zero hips, and she wore an orange tank top that exposed her toned and tanned arms. "What are you wearing? A doll's dress? I want a picture of this!"

She fumbled into her bag for her camera. "Perfect for Facebook," she said, scrambling and searching wildly for the object that Aurora prayed she wouldn't find.

"Hi, Hattie." Aurora's voice trembled, and she searched the backyard for an escape route. Jonathan Stockington though only seventeen, was preoccupied chugging a beer that he most likely stole from Hattie's parents' fridge. His blond hair was drenched from the pool water and tied back in a ponytail.

"Wuz up, Aurora?" he said, smiling like he was posing for *GQ* magazine. His chest was bare and dripping with sweat that streamed down his defined chest. His only article of clothing was a fiery red bathing suit that clung to his masculine body, and Aurora had to stop herself from gaping at him. She wished it was her arm he clung to and not Hattie's.

"Hi, Jonathan," she said softly, her voice sounding as if it was swallowed in their presence.

"Look at her dress, Jonathan. It's hideous on her."

"I don't see anything wrong with it," he said, chugging again and squeezing the can in his hand so that it crumpled into a disfigured shape. "You've worn tighter things than that."

"Well, I can. There's a difference. What a bore this block party is. Let's get out of here and go back to my place. The parents are all getting drunk out here."

"But the baseball game's about to start, baby. They want me to be the starting pitcher."

"I'm sure you'll be great," Aurora said, smiling too brightly, and Hattie noticed from the corner of her eye.

"You wouldn't turn down some alone time with me for a stupid baseball game. I mean it's not even for the high school team."

"Why can't I do both?" He took a step back, going into his pitcher stance. Then he swung his arm back and released his hand, moving closer and closer toward Hattie until he ended up pinching her backside.

Hattie squealed in delight and made sure that Aurora was watching. "Please, Jonathan, not here. I don't want Little Miss Straight-A Student here to go squealing to my mom like a little pig."

"I won't do that," Aurora stammered, staring down at her blue loafers that were not as cool as Hattie's silver strappy sandals.

"Cool it, Hattie," Jonathan said, tossing the empty beer can toward the recycle bin. It ricocheted off the sides like a boomerang. "If you want to get out of here, then let's go. I won't go to the game."

"That's a good boy." She smiled and let out a victorious high-pitched laugh. Then she maliciously pointed her manicured claws at Aurora as if they would scratch her. Smiling her mischievous grin, she called out loud and clear so everyone within earshot could hear her.

"Mr. Stockington, make sure you put on extra burgers. Aurora is here. There might not be enough for the rest of us."

Aurora felt her eyes welling up with tears as she looked back at the gloating face of Hattie and the face of Jonathan, who shook his head, disgusted, and started tugging on Hattie to get her alone with him. Aurora felt like her buttons were popping off her dress and that she was exposed in front of the entire block party. She felt her head throbbing as she stood there mortified, tightening her clutch on her purse.

Everyone in the front yard was now pointing and staring at her. She heard some of her classmates laughing, chanting *Fatty Alvarez* in unison. She hated them. She thought she saw one snap a picture of her. She looked up, and it was Boreas who had snapped it on his cell phone camera. She didn't know what got into her, but she snatched the cell phone out of his unexpected grasp and flung it against a tree trunk so that it smashed into pieces. Boreas scrambled to pick up the damaged pieces and cursed at her when he realized there was no hope to fix it.

"You'll pay for this," he cried out.

Stunned and shaken, Aurora turned and ran as fast as she could in shock and despair, dropping Old Mr. Harold's hamburger as an innocent casualty. She ran through the backwoods, not caring that her dress was torn mercilessly by branches. She was not going back to the block party or to Wishbone Avenue ever again. She didn't care what her mother said. She was going to hide and never come out. She couldn't believe she had made such a fool of herself in front of Jonathan. And Hattie was the one kissing him, the one holding him and making love to him. She felt the rage within her make her run faster, the trees whirling past her until she collapsed and cried, her face buried in the grass to muffle her sobs. She didn't care what time it was or who would be looking for her. She doubted anyone even missed her. Aurora was an embarrassment to the Alvarez family, nothing like the legacy her mother had made in this town. Her mother shouldn't have had a daughter like her.

Aurora felt sick to her stomach, her body convulsing as she sobbed harder and harder. Night was encroaching over Candlewick, the trees acting as a canopy. The sunset painted the sky with an abundance of colors stretching out toward the sobbing girl hidden beneath the comforting arms of the tree branches. Aurora didn't even notice time drifting forward as she was immersed in her frozen moment of grief, crying until she passed out, the stars her only witness as the tears were absorbed into the earth.

Chapter 4

The Unveiling

A urora awoke to the blast of fireworks in the air as the colors streamed across the sky. She jumped up, frazzled and disoriented, trying to get her bearings before finally discerning she was still in the backwoods behind Mrs. Taboo's ruby-red house. She took a deep breath, wiped the dirt and tears away from her eyes, and paused to reflect on what she was going to do now. The fireworks show had started, and nobody had cared to look for her. She was invisible.

Aurora leaned against the side of the house to fix her shoe that was untied. The events of that afternoon made her nauseous, and she could not face these people again. Not Hattie, not Jonathan or her mother or Boreas, who would most likely make her pay for his broken cell phone. She wished she could stay hidden in those back-woods forever, but the night was making her restless and uneasy, especially being so close to the mysterious ruby-red house, where the inhabitants were never exposed. They were hidden away just like she was.

She stared at the house now within her touch and she felt fear gnawing at her intestines and she started imagining shadows coming to life and encircling her. She removed her hand from the wooden paneling and retraced her steps to go unnoticed from this forbidden abyss. She started to break out into a run when all of a sudden the deep blowing of the conch shell sounded out of nowhere, and she froze mid-step. She felt like her feet were glued to the soil, and her body trembled as she slowly turned to face the house that without a doubt was the source of this mysterious sound. She thought her mind was playing more tricks on her because out of the darkness one of the shadows had in fact come to life and was heading straight toward her. Overcome with fear, the shadow advanced, coming closer and closer. She braced herself for impact as the shadow collided with her body and both tumbled to the ground.

"Ow!" It exclaimed. "What the hell!"

It was a boy's voice, and Aurora stood up quickly in defensive stance, groaning slightly from the ache the impact had left in her side. "Who is there?" she said forcefully, her voice no longer paralyzed.

The figure struggled to its feet and rubbed its knees. "You're that stupid girl who broke my phone!" it shouted at her. "I've been looking for you all afternoon. You owe me a new phone!"

Of all the people to run into in the woods it had to be Boreas Stockington.

"Look, I'm sorry about your phone. I will get you a new one."

"You'd better! And I am going to sue you for attacking me!"

"You can't sue me for attacking you. You attacked me. You rammed right into me."

"I thought you were a tree."

"I look nothing like a tree."

"Well, a very demented-looking tree."

Another firecracker went off by the Stockington house, exploding shades of bright orange and yellows into the night sky, their twinkling resembling fallen stars.

"What are you doing here anyway?" Aurora asked as she rubbed her side, convinced it would be bruised by the Awakened Hour. She wished she had some ice. "Aren't you supposed to be with your family, lighting the fireworks for the grand finale?"

Boreas swayed back and forth, and Aurora's eyes began adjusting to the darkness and making out more than the shadowed frame of the teenager in front of her.

"They are doing fine without me," he said sternly. "And it's none of your business why I'm here."

"Sorry. I didn't mean to piss you off."

"You already mastered that by breaking my phone."

"Then you shouldn't have taken that picture of me, you jerk," she exclaimed, nearly pushing him, but he backed up out of her reach.

"What picture?"

"You heard me!"

Just then the conch shell sounded in the night, and both Boreas and Aurora froze, listening to the sound now getting louder and clearer in their midst.

"Did you hear...?"

"Yeah! Wait, you really did?"

"Yeah. I thought I was going crazy."

"Me too!"

It sounded again, this time stronger and steadier.

Aurora felt goose bumps prickle on the back of her neck. "It's coming from the house."

"But no one lives there. My dad said it was abandoned months ago."

"Old Mr. Harold said he saw Mrs. Taboo last week, that she still lives there."

"Old Mr. Harold is a quack."

"Then are we quacks too?"

One lone broken shutter banged against the side of the house, causing Aurora's heart to nearly burst out of her chest. She was very glad Boreas had turned up when he did, though of course she would never admit it out loud. She watched as the leaves of the honey locust trees gently swayed back and forth in the wind. An outsider would never suspect that thorns lay hidden beneath those leaves, spiking out on the branches. Aurora feared this ruby-red house was just like those trees—appearing all innocent but potential danger within. And yet despite her instincts telling her to retreat, the answer was as clear to her as it had been that morning.

"We have to go into the house," she declared, and Boreas laughed at her.

"You got to be kidding. I am not going in there. It's probably haunted or some crazy perverts are trying to lure us into their cave."

"You watch a lot of movies, don't you?"

"Well, there is some foundation of truth in that. My body is telling me to run—adrenaline pumping and all that scientific crap. You cannot be seriously thinking we need to go in there."

"Did you hear the conch shell last night at the Sacred Hour?"

Boreas turned to her in complete disbelief. "How did you know that? Are you in cahoots with whatever is in there?"

"No, you idiot. I heard it too. And I heard it sound my name. It's calling us. For some reason only we can hear this, and whatever is inside needs our help."

Boreas gulped and nodded. "Well, then ladies first."

The wind howled as they took their first steps toward the little ruby-red house, their footsteps crunching the grass with each step they took. Ghoulish faces were imprinted onto the tree trunks and glared at them as they trespassed. The sky was slightly overcast so that the only light was from the occasional burst of a firework that exploded nearby. It highlighted enough of the path before them to help them reach the window without tripping over the loose roots that were sticking out from the ground like booby traps barricading their path.

"I don't think we should do this," Boreas whispered, his deep voice pleading. "My dad will literally kill me if I end up in Candlewick Prison again."

"Shhh," she instructed urgently as she mimed to him to give her a boost with his hands in order to reach the window. "Just don't look up my dress," she warned, and he snickered as if that was the last thing on his mind. Cobwebs draped over the crevice of the window, but it was slightly open, just enough to squeeze her pinky finger underneath and pull upward with all her strength. At first it didn't budge, and a mosquito buzzed around her ear, distracting her momentarily. Boreas held her feet in his palms and whispered to her that it was possibly rusted from lack of use.

"Try again," he urged, struggling to keep his balance.

She took a deep breath, mustering as much energy as she could, and lifted again with all her strength. The window squeaked slightly and then gave way, and she was able to squeeze the rest of her hands underneath and pull upward, creating an opening just big enough for the two of them to squeeze through. She wished she had changed out of her torn dress because jeans and a t-shirt would have made this break-in much more manageable. Burglars did not go breaking into people's houses while wearing tight dresses. Probably rule number one in the guidebooks.

Her eyes adjusted to the darkness, and it appeared she was looking at a dining room. A table setting was placed at the head of the table, but it was clear of food. She smelled pea soup, but the plates were clean. Whoever was about to eat had lost their appetite in a hurry or was still cooking in the other room. She spotted a small flashlight on the table and hoped it would still work.

"Boreas, I think I see a flashlight. I am going to go first. If I am not out in ten minutes, call the police."

"With what? I don't have a phone, remember?"

Aurora wanted to kick him but instead tossed him her purse. "My phone's in there. I don't have a lot of battery, so don't turn it on unless you absolutely have to. I'll be right out."

"Don't get caught," he whispered, the wind carrying the panic in his voice, which added to the feelings of foreboding she was experiencing first hand.

She slipped through the window and landed on the carpeted rug of the ruby-red house, picking up the small flashlight sitting on the cabinet. She was an unwelcome visitor, and the house knew it. She tiptoed her way across the carpeted dining room floor and pressed her ear against the closed mahogany door. The disturbing scent of pea soup wafted through the slits in the door, but she could not make out any motion or sound from within. She fumbled in the darkness for the door knob and opened it a crack. The door made a screeching sound, like a tortured cat screaming in slow motion, but there was no turning back. Aurora flung the door open and pressed her shaking finger onto the rubbery knob of the flashlight, and to her relief it illuminated a yellowish halo over a dilapidated kitchen. A wretchedly old and weathered pot was sitting on the stove. The gas burner was turned off but the scent of soup was still potent and rancid. She wearily turned around expecting at any minute the chef to pop out from behind the closed doors and make his or her where-abouts known. She had to stay in control of her senses and stay in the moment. There was someone living in this house after all. Soup had been made, but the chef had disappeared. Why? Was it before or after the conch shell had sounded and called them to this spot? She wanted to call out but didn't know if Mrs. Taboo would appreciate her trespassing. Maybe she should have tried the doorbell first. That would have been logical. Why did she sense that the conch shell owner was in trouble? And what could she, an overweight girl of fifteen, who knew one self-defense move that her gym teacher had taught them the year before, do about it? Old Mr. Harold described Mrs. Taboo as an old woman. If that was the case, Aurora thought she could probably take her—as long as Old Mr. Harold was not senile.

She meandered her way slowly past the kitchen and into the foyer that led to the living room. Cobwebs draped down from the ceiling and the couches were smothered with dusty old sheets, as if it had been uninhabited for months. An old grandfather clock was silent in the corner, the hands fastened to the Sacred Hour. Dust tickled her nostrils, and she had to squeeze her nose so that she didn't sneeze and bring down the entire house. She felt the floor was swaying—or was her mind hallucinating? She followed the mustard-yellow carpet that led her to a narrow corridor with medieval paintings fastened to the walls. She saw one of a cross and peered at it most curiously. The symbol of Christianity. She recalled reading about it in online by the author Thomas Young. He had been arrested after getting the story through the government security censures and had found a way to distribute the story to whoever had been online at that moment. Aurora had been one of those people and had read the story about a man named Jesus who could perform miracles. He had died for the people's sins. Aurora had read the story, fascinated, but thinking it very farfetched. Immediately after the release, Thomas Young had disappeared, never to be heard from again, and the story was destroyed out of her inbox. But they hadn't found a way to destroy her memory.

Aurora finally reached the end of the hall where there was only one more room left to view. The door was shut, and she hoped that her heartbeat was not audible to anyone besides herself. It was eerily quiet except for the nasally soft breaths she was taking, and she had a strong urge to flee from this place. There was something not right, and she feared what lay behind this sealed shut door, her imagination thinking of all different obscene scenarios. Maybe there was a reason this door was shut. People didn't just leave their doors closed all the time. Could the inhabitants have been poisoned or killed by an insane madman who'd dumped their bodies in the bedroom?

Once again her curiosity led to excitement and renewed strength, and she slowly reached down with a quivering hand and touched the metallic knob, sparks bursting from her skin. She shook her hand and realized the static shock must have been from treading over the carpet. She tried again, and this time her hand enclosed the door knob with no obstructive force. She counted to ten and turned it quickly, shining the light into the darkness. An old woman's gray eyes stared back at her, and Aurora screamed at the top of her lungs, her cry echoing throughout the entire house. She slammed the door shut and backed up against the wall, shrieking again, as the entire house appeared to come to life. She fell to the ground, searching wildly for the flashlight she had dropped. Where was it? She feared the door would fling open and the old woman's eyes would again peer directly into her own. She put her hand against something hard, but it wasn't a flashlight. She traced it with her hands and then realized it was a foot! A hand reached down and grabbed her shoulder. Instinctively she punched with all her strength and jumped to her feet, hearing the groans of her attacker. She then immediately performed her one self-defense move, which was putting her attacker into a head lock.

"Aurora," the voice gasped. "It's me! It's me!"

She immediately released her hold on Boreas, recognizing his voice. He coughed again and again, his body letting air flow back into his bronchial passages.

"Are you trying to kill me?" he shrieked, leaning against the wall.

"I thought you were trying to kill me! What are you doing here? I thought you were standing guard!"

The flashlight was piercing his eyes, and he grabbed it from out of her hand. "Don't shine that thing at me. You screamed, and I came rushing in to make sure you were okay. What happened?"

"I got scared. I thought it was Mrs. Taboo."

She opened the door, this time in one fluid motion, and shone the light on the eyes of the old woman, this time the light illuminated the rest of the canvas.

"It's just a painting of her. But that's all that's there. There are no more rooms in the house and it's definitely uninhabited. If someone lived here they would have heard my scream. The conch shell must have been a trick or maybe even an animal from the woods."

"An animal that sounds like a conch shell?" Boreas shook his head, not convinced.

He opened the bedroom door and shone the light on the painting of Mrs. Taboo. She was Indian and dressed in a red sari with a shawl draped over her head. She was holding a compass that pointed north. She had a wicked smile on her wrinkled and withered face. The painting was held up against the wall over the bed that didn't appear to have been slept in for weeks.

"It doesn't add up," Boreas said. "Then who made the soup?"

"Must have been from Mrs. Taboo when she came back. Over a week ago. That's why it smells so rancid, left out in this heat for all that time."

"And the rats," Boreas cried out. Both immediately jumped to the opposite sides of the room as a large furry gray rat scurried past them. Aurora had her hand to her mouth to muffle her shriek. She was through with this house of horrors. She grabbed the flashlight from Boreas's hand and started to retreat out of the bedroom when all of a sudden the conch shell sounded again, this time louder and clearer than it had before.

"It's coming from behind the painting," Aurora shouted, madly jumping onto the bed and lunging for the painting. "Someone is trapped behind it."

Boreas bounded onto the bed, and both tried pulling the painting off its hinge, the old woman's crooked smile gloating at them as if she knew something they didn't.

"It's not coming off. What kind of painting is this?"

She started banging on the wall and screaming, "We are here. Can you hear us? We can't get the painting off."

"I'll run and get help," Boreas shouted, about to jump off the bed when the entire house shook like an earthquake. They tumbled violently off the bed. Furniture crashed to the ground and sunk beneath the floor like quicksand, sucking everything in. Glass broke around them as the room started caving in. Aurora tried to cling onto the bedpost, but a shelf knocked into her and caused her to lose her grip and she slid toward the black hole vortex.

"I am going to fall under," Aurora exclaimed, feeling her weight being pulled down beneath the floor boards. Boreas grabbed her hand and tried to hold onto the bedpost with the other. The pressure was unbearable, beating down on them.

"I can't hold on much longer," he said, watching her head sinking beneath the crevice of the ground.

All of a sudden another shake caused his hand to loosen its grip, and they both tumbled beneath the bedroom floorboards, falling into the abyss.

Chapter 5

Otus

Aurora fell through the black hole as if she was a dead weight with no control over her fate, no control over whether she lived or died. As she fell her mind was a blur of images replaying over and over as she tumbled through the dark abyss—of her father reading his magazine, her mother smiling in her dandelion dress. Aurora feared what her parents would say when they didn't find her later that night. Would they miss her? Would they know how much she loved them? She clutched for anything to prevent her fall, reaching out into blind space and praying for something to materialize out of nothing. And then it felt as if she was standing still while the rest of the world was spinning out of control. She still held Boreas's hand as they were free falling through the center of the earth. She spotted a light below her and knew that this was the end. She closed her eyes, expecting the impact to strike, but instead of her body plummeting against cement or gravel, she bounced on something soft and springy. She started bouncing again and again on the strange soft cushion, and her body levitated upward to start the bungee jumping motion over again. Her stomach retched and she felt queasy as she bounced once again into the air; her hand separated from Boreas's grasp. She wondered if this was what death was like: bouncing up and down through eternity.

She opened her eyes, and her mouth dropped in disbelief as she beheld this parallel universe. They had been sucked into an identical replica of the ruby-red cottage bedroom, except this one was nearly three times the size of the first one. This dreamlike existence was euphoric, and she continued bouncing on the bed until she lost momentum and flung herself down, kissing the piece of furniture that had saved her life. She stood up and surveyed the large white mattress that stretched for fifty meters in each direction. She spotted Boreas, hunched on his side in the fetal position. She tried to run to him but found it more feasible to skip to him, attempting to maintain balance and not topple over. She reached his side and started shaking him wildly in an attempt to wake him up.

"Boreas, we're alive!"

His eyelids fluttered open at the sound of her voice; his eyes appeared dazed and confused as they surveyed this world around them.

"This is all your fault."

"My fault! Did you not hear what I said? We're alive!"

He stood up on the giant mattress. "You call this being alive? We're like in some messed up parallel universe!"

His sudden movements caused the mattress to start to sway, and she had to hop slightly as if trapped on a trampoline.

"What is this place?" she asked, surveying their surroundings. "I have never seen or read about anything like this in our history books or magazines."

"Well, I can tell you that we are both completely insane. The school therapist would tell me I have lost all sense of reality and am schizophrenic. None of this is real. You are not even real."

Aurora ignored him and started to explore the edge of the mattress. "I feel real," she thought half humorously.

Suddenly their bodies fell victim to the vibrations of the conch shell sounding, causing the entire bed to shake and their eardrums to nearly burst. It was like another earthquake was shaking the mattress causing it to rise like the ebb and flow of oceanic waves. Boreas and Aurora plunged head first into the mattress and started to flip over, doing somersaults like two puppets on a string. Aurora sensed danger approaching, and fear seized her from the inside out. A large shadow inched over the white mattress, towering over them like a fast-approaching storm cloud. Aurora and Boreas strained their necks, following the shadow as they covered their ears as tight as they could as the cacophonous symphony continued to play.

Aurora screamed out, "Please stop!"

The conch shell immediately ceased playing. The two bodies flung face first in a downward dive and crashed against the mattress as the shadow lingered over them.

A deep voice bellowed, "Aurora? Boreas?"

Aurora was frozen in fear as she turned over onto her back and looked up into the eyes of an enormously tall giant! He stood over her at thirty feet tall, with gangling arms and a large, thick neck like a dinosaur. He wore old blue overalls with both pant legs too short, exposing feet the size of a tugboat. Though his body was gigantic in proportion to the two teenagers, his face was youthful with bright green eyes and large cheekbones. He had thick, furry eyebrows that arched down toward his rotund nose. He held the conch shell in his burly hand that could crush them both with one downward pulsating thrust.

Boreas and Aurora screamed as the giant hovered above them. The giant screamed back at them, horrified by their reaction, and fell backward onto the floor, hiding unsuccessfully behind the bed frame. Aurora turned to Boreas with a mixture of terror and curiosity, and then she cautiously leaned over the side of the bed to see the giant covering his face with his hands. His enormous green eye peeked out through the crevice between his giant middle and pointer fingers. He appeared more scared than she felt, despite being more than five times her size.

"Don't be afraid," she stammered. "I am Aurora. And this is my friend Boreas. You're the one who played the conch shell, aren't you?"

He nodded twice, his hair sweeping itself over his pale forehead, and his hands slid down his face and folded themselves over his broad chest.

"I am sorry. I didn't know how else to get you down here. I hope I didn't scare you."

"You bet your life you scared us!" Boreas exclaimed, pulling a Swiss army knife out of his pocket and holding the blade up so that the giant could see it. From that perspective it must have appeared like a child's toy. "Now you take us back to Earth this instant or else."

"Put that away." Aurora scolded, wondering why she was all of a sudden comfortable with this gigantic teenager.

"I knew you would come! I knew you would come save me after I heard your voice." His thick, chubby finger pointed down at Aurora, who nodded slightly.

"Who are you?" she asked, again rising to her feet to get a better look at him.

"I am called Otus."

Boreas snickered. "Who names their child Otus?"

"Who names one son Jonathan and the next son Boreas?"

"My dead mother, that's who, so thank you for bringing up that painful memory."

Aurora wanted to pull her hair out in aggravation. "I apologize, Otus, for my friend here. Actually, he's not even my friend. We sort of just ran into each other."

"After she destroyed my cell phone."

Otus watched them mystified as they bantered back and forth, excitement evident in his face as these two visitors were squabbling before him. "Cell phones? What are they?"

Boreas pulled Aurora's cell phone out of his pocket. "I forgot we had this. We might get reception down here, wherever we are." He got up and bounced around the bed, trying to get reception. "Nothing. Not even a single bar. Where the hell are we?"

"Underneath the house, of course," Otus laughed, watching Boreas. "Is that a magical communication device?"

Boreas bounded back over toward Otus and then sat with his legs suspended over the side of the bed. He suspiciously stared at Otus but then in a macho manner thrust the phone over in his direction without the nerve to hand it to him. "Here, giant. Maybe with your height you can get some reception."

Otus cradled the cell phone in his palm like a fragile child. He tried to press the buttons, but his fingers were too thick, so he just slid his finger over the surface and admired the lights. "What an extraordinary invention. What does it do?"

"It is through satellite, and you can call people. Everyone has their own unique telephone number, and you can dial it and talk to them over the phone. You can also take pictures and text people."

Boreas continued to ramble on and on like a salesman, and Otus nodded, absorbing this information with delight written all over his face.

"I wish I could have this. I wish I could have a lot of things." He handed the phone back to Aurora then eyed his two visitors. "Are you hungry? I have some rat stew that I made."

Aurora and Boreas both made faces of complete disgust, but Otus didn't notice and scampered off like an excited child about to do show and tell with the class.

"Let's get out of here." Boreas nudged Aurora hurriedly. "Quick, while he is in the other room."

Aurora stood up and surveyed the bedroom around them. There was a large desk and chair as well as the humongous painting of the old woman, Mrs. Taboo; her eyes even more menacing as a larger adaptation.

"We fell through there," she pointed upward toward the zenith, where there was a small black dot in the ceiling. "That's the way we need to go."

Boreas tried bouncing on the bed as high as he could but was not even anywhere close to the ceiling. "How are we going to get out of here?"

Aurora heard the giant's footsteps approaching and grabbed Boreas so that they were both seated side by side again on the bed. "Just follow my lead," she commanded.

Otus returned holding a large pot of some ghoulish rat stew that he stirred with a wooden spoon. The smell reminded Aurora of the old city subway, and she had to prevent herself from gagging.

"I am not much of a cook, but I had to learn on my own. I make such dishes as spider burgers, soufflé a la worm, maggot pie, and cockroach crunch cereal."

He dished out three bowls' worth of the rats stew with tails hanging over the edges of the bowls. Aurora had to bite her tongue as he placed the beach ball-sized bowls beside the visitors. They peered in as the steam caused them both to suffer from coughing fits. The rat's tail as a garnish looked as if it would start swinging back and forth at any moment.

Aurora, though extremely hungry, did not have enough of an appetite to embark on trying this new dish. Boreas was waiting for her cue as Otus handed him a spoon and urged him to try first.

"You're going to love it."

Boreas dipped the spoon into the bowl and lifted a small amount of broth that sat swimming in the cylinder. Otus smiling wider and wider as Boreas tried to lift it. He then dropped it like a weight, dismissing it as too heavy for him.

Otus dipped it once again into the bubbling substance and lifted the spoon to Boreas's lips, feeding him. Boreas's eyes darted to Aurora, who had lost her train of thought, entranced by this feeding session happening as if she was at the zoo. Boreas opened his mouth a smidgeon and slurped the broth down, swallowing quickly and wiping his mouth with the back of his sleeve. He started panting and spitting but then froze and looked up at the horrified face of Otus.

"Yum," Boreas smiled sheepishly, licking his lips.

Otus threw the bowl against the wall, the dead rat flying out of the bowl and slithering down the wall.

"This was a mistake," he scowled bitterly.

"You can't take offense with Boreas. He liked the soup. Didn't you, Boreas?" Aurora nudged Boreas, who quickly agreed.

Otus slumped down on the chair and pulled out the conch shell. Both teens cowered down, fearful he would blow it again and cause another earthquake. "The last time I had a visitor was the old woman."

"Mrs. Taboo," Aurora said, pointing to the picture.

"That's the woman who hid me away. She tried to help me when no one else did. Her last gift was this conch shell. She didn't tell me where she got it but said that whoever heard this sound would help me. I would find the Goddess of Dawn and the God of the North Wind, and together we would travel to the Aurora Borealis. Only through them would the spirits of the past rekindle hope for the future."

"Aurora Borealis?" Boreas asked, perplexed.

"The northern lights," Aurora said slowly. "My father told me about them once. You can see this natural phenomenon at the magnetic pole, and they illuminate the northern horizon as a greenish glow or even at times like a reddish color, emulating the sun rising. The auroras were commonly believed to be a sign from God and have had a number of names throughout history, but in the 1600s a man named Pierre Gassendi named the effect of these northern lights after the Roman Goddess of Dawn, Aurora, and the Greek God of the North Wind, Boreas.

"Aurora Borealis," Otus repeated, listening intently to the history.

"Yeah, but today scientists have proven that they are caused mainly due to the collision of energetic, charged particles with atoms in the high atmosphere."

Boreas stared at her like she had three heads. "Did you understand anything that came out of your mouth?"

Otus stood up, clutching the conch shell in his hands. "Do you know about a Geometric Storm?"

"I don't know anything about a Geometric Storm," Aurora replied faintly, watching him advancing toward her as if he was ready to crush her with his mighty fist. "I mean, we can find out. There are books at the library. Maybe there is a way that we can get in to find out more."

Otus picked her up, and Aurora screamed at the top of her voice. Boreas kicked the monster with all his force, but the giant didn't flinch. Otus lifted her up toward his mouth, salivating, and her body went numb in his hands. He then kissed her on the top of her hair and laughed outright. "I knew you were the right Aurora."

"I am not the right Aurora. I just have the same name. I am no Goddess of Dawn. I am..." she felt the room spinning wildly around her, and he patted her on the head again.

"Soon you'll know who you really are," he smiled, putting her back down on the ground. "As for you Boreas, we will see about you. You did eat the soup. You must be braver than we think. And first impressions could be deceiving. Now let's get out of here."

He walked over to the picture of Mrs. Taboo and opened it, revealing a hidden dark tunnel within. He snatched up his two travelling companions and placed them into his overalls pocket near his heart, which was thumping like a loud metronome. They observed the tunnel, which led upward; a light was visible at the end like a beacon of hope. They were to travel through this secret underground tunnel leading them out of the giant realm and back into the town of Candlewick, which appeared to be five miles away. Otus proceeded to climb up the metal rods of the tunnel toward the beacon of light, slowly and steadily. Aurora continued to think about everything that they had just heard from the giant in order to get her mind off the impending doom that was in store for her or Boreas if they fell out of the pocket and tumbled to their demise.

"The Candlewick Library will probably have information about the Geometric Storm," Aurora said thinking out loud, trying hard not to look down. "But there's no way that we will be allowed in. The library has been forbidden to everyone except the Common Good government officials."

"What's so important about this Geometric Storm anyway?" Boreas asked, clasping the overall fabric even tighter as they were suspended facing the spiraling tunnel beneath them.

"That's the storm that will cause cataclysmic damage to this planet. Mrs. Taboo said that it will be worse than a hundred nuclear bombs going off simultaneously."

"When do you think the next one will be?"

"She didn't say."

"Where is Mrs. Taboo? Did she get captured by the Inspector?" Aurora asked, holding on for dear life and praying that the stitches of this overalls pocket would not rip.

"She had to return to help the people who built this underground room. They had built it to keep me safe until I found the two of you. Mrs. Taboo and her party."

"Like the Common Good Party?" Boreas chimed in.

"No, more like the Spiritual Party. Mrs. Taboo believes that I am on this Earth at this time for a reason, that I am the answer to a prophecy, meant to save this world. They predicted that I would be found by the Goddess of Dawn and the God of the North Wind… and here you are."

"Um, I am not some God of the North Wind," Boreas laughed and then held on tighter as Otus took a large leap from one ladder rung to the next. "Besides, why would you need two humans to stop this storm when you are a giant? Where are your other giant pals to help you?"

Otus took a deep sigh and said, "According to Mrs. Taboo, I am the last of my kind to actually help the human race. I did have a brother once. Ephialtes. But he thought giants were superior to humans and that he could force them to do his bidding. I had to stop him, and by doing so I had to destroy the only family I had left. Mrs. Taboo was the only human friend I had, and she helped me outwit him. Afterward she told me I am meant for a great quest, and then she brought me here to Candlewick."

Boreas turned toward Aurora, mouthing to her that they were in big trouble. Aurora nodded feeling her heartbeat racing as all of this felt like some deranged dream that she was not waking up from. Once again curiosity was getting the best of her and she wanted to find out more about Otus and this Geometric Storm. If the answers were in the Candlewick Library then she could at least try to help Otus and still get home before curfew. Her parents were probably thinking that she was still at the fireworks show or at the barbeque. She fumbled for her cell phone and couldn't believe it was almost the Sacred Hour. Time had seemed to stand still in the basement, but to her dismay it had sped up.

They reached the end of the tunnel, and Aurora feared that they would be exposed as soon as they were back in the real world.

"You'll be seen!" she exclaimed, horrified. "You can't just walk around Candlewick. This will cause a panic of catastrophic proportions."

Otus laughed heartily and then put his hands on the circular door that resembled a metallic sewer cover.

"I'd have to be standing still for that to happen. Now at the count of three we all have to put our hands on the imprints on the metallic casing or else this journey will be cut short."

On the metallic casing were two large handprints that matched the size and shape of Otus's hands. Then there were two sets of hand prints that were engraved into the metal. One was the size of Boreas's hands and the other matched Aurora's. Together they stared at this metallic casing, and Otus placed the two teenagers on the top of his head to be able to reach it. They sat on the soft strands of his hair and reached up to fit their hands into the pre-destined hand prints. Once all three had their hands together they pushed upward, and the casing gave way.

"It worked!" Otus cried out, so excited that Aurora and Boreas nearly flew off the top of his head and clung onto strands of his hair for dear life. He immediately caught them and placed them safely back into the pocket of his overalls.

"Oops, sorry about that. Need to remember that you aren't giants like me. Now hang on."

Like a gas explosion, the metal cover shot up into the air, and Otus flew up with it. Otus took long leaps into the air, going faster than the speed of light. If someone did see Otus, it would be in mid-blink, and then they would assume they were seeing things, if they even pondered it at all. Boreas and Aurora gaped down at their town in disbelief as they were hurled up. The town resembled miniature dollhouses from the height they reached, nearly as high as the clouds. The pressure was astronomical in the atmosphere, but they were going so fast that their bodies were quickly restored to their natural pressure and gravity levels each time they were suspended in midair. It was almost like being sucked into a vacuum and released so quickly that the body didn't have a chance to react.

"Woohoo!" Otus cried out into the atmosphere. "And you both thought I was a crazy oaf of a giant. I may be. Or I may be much more. Now grab on tighter. Time to leave the burrows of the earth and make our way toward the lights."

Chapter 6

Breaking the Rules

"*T*here's no connection between our names and the northern lights! It is purely a coincidence."

"What if there is no such thing as a coincidence? We are the only ones who could hear the conch shell."

Aurora and Boreas were in the Candlewick Private Library, having broken in with the help of their new travelling companion. Boreas had disabled the security camera as Otus stood watch outside since he was unable to fit into the miniature library due to his giant proportions. The two teenagers were now in a desperate search for information about the Geometric Storm.

"He's a nutcase," Boreas exclaimed, throwing another book on the pile. "I can't believe he said that Mrs. Taboo belongs to a spiritual party. I thought all religions were abolished by the Common Good Party."

"I guess there are still people working underground."

Boreas and Aurora continued to search through the mounds of books for any reference to a Geometric Storm, but were coming up empty. Guilt gnawed at Aurora's throat as she kept reminding herself that she was in the library illegally. Books were no longer available to the public, except for government-mandated textbooks used for teaching. Everything else could be found online. However, the problem with the material on the Internet was that everything was censored by the Common Good Party. If anyone had an opinion that differed from the Common Good, it was immediately taken down and destroyed. The people had agreed to this when the IDEAL had come to power fifteen years earlier.

Aurora held one of these rare relics, now a museum piece to be observed and never read. She ran her finger down the spine of the book and opened the thick cover to behold the yellowed pages within. Dust filled her nostrils, and she sneezed, fearful that she had awakened the silent books in this mausoleum. She cautiously turned the yellowed pages, expecting the paper to combust in her hand. She didn't understand how something this small could be so damaging.

"Wait, what is this?" Boreas whispered, thrusting a magazine article in her face.

Aurora picked up the magazine, and there in black and white was a picture of Mrs. Xiomy, their high school science teacher. She was around the age of twenty-one, wearing a shawl that covered the top of her head and wrapped around her shoulders. There was a look of pure agony on her face as she reached out toward a man being led away by two police officers in handcuffs, his back to the camera. Falling from her hand was a protest sign that read "Abolish IDEAL! Keep Freedom for All!"

"She was a protestor," Aurora said, astounded.

"Still as beautiful then as she is now!" he sighed, drooling over the picture.

Aurora grabbed the picture from his hands, aggravated. "Can we stay focused, Boreas?"

"Oh, um, yeah."

He shuffled his chair, turning a shade of mauve, and Aurora proceeded with reading the article. *Since the Common Good won the majority party in government, their followers have already begun tearing down signs of churches, mosques, temples, and other places of worship and converting them into IDEAL meeting houses. The Religious Protest leader, IMAM, has been arrested as he attempted to barricade the doors of St. Patrick's Cathedral in New York City along with several followers. IMAM, also known as the rebel David Xiomy, got into a confrontation with one of the officers and construction workers looking to tear down the building. This lead to a brawl that resulted in fifteen killed and forty arrested.Without its leader, the organization has been dissolved, and the Common Good has finally declared to loud pandemonium and cheer that after two years of unrest and war, freedom of religion has been abolished. A brighter future has been initiated for all in the newly established United States of the Common Good.*

The two teenagers finished reading the article but continued staring down at the pages and the picture of their teacher reaching out toward David Xiomy, her husband.

"I think we just opened Pandora's box," Aurora whispered, fear resonated in her chest as she stared into Boreas's eyes. Before he could respond, the sound of keys jangling broke the silence. Aurora quickly ripped the newspaper article out of the archives and stuffed it into her bag, and Boreas switched off the flashlight. They stood there like two defenseless mice about to be caught by the hungry cat.

The door creaked open, and two high beams of orange light pierced through the darkness of the library. The beams were followed by heavy footsteps emerging into the sanctuary.

A voice with a thick Brooklyn accent boomed out, "Where you at, kiddies? We know you're in here."

A husky female voice sounded after him along with a bang as she hit her partner with the flashlight. "Woolchuck, cut it out. You sound like you're a dog catcher."

"Dog catcher. Common Good officer. Same thing. We are both out to nab someone or something. Pelican, do you have a better idea?"

"Well, now they know we're here," the female exclaimed, disgruntled, as she shone her flashlight in a multitude of directions. "I am Officer Pelican. You thought you were slick disabling the security camera, but that didn't stop the floor tracking device from going off at headquarters."

"Yeah, you're both busted, so let's make this easy for us all. Come out slowly with your hands up, and no one is going to get hurt."

Boreas and Aurora slowly inched backward hiding behind a large shelf that was labeled the Travel Section. Crouched down, they huddled in the darkness as the light beams went from shelf to shelf. The front door was about fifty yards away, and the police officers had locked it in order to barricade their escape. Aurora squeezed her head in between two books and saw a window that she might be able to use to signal to Otus that they were in danger. However, one of the officers was standing right in front of it.

"I need to get to that window," she whispered to Boreas.

"I'll create a diversion," he whispered back, taking a peek to see that the coast was clear and then making a mad dash for the shelves parallel to the Travel Section. Aurora watched him in awe as his tennis skills kicked him. He zigzagged from one shelf to the next on the balls of his feet, just being missed by the high beams of light. The book she had been leaning on started to slide out of its nook, and she caught it right before it was about to plunge against the floor and reveal her whereabouts.

"Cursed book!" she whispered, aggravated with herself but relieved by her reflexes. The title of the book was *Alaska Uncovered,* and her heart stopped, wondering if there could be something about the Aurora Borealis in that book and the mysterious Geometric Storm. She stuffed it into her bag and peered out through the crack of the book shelf. Boreas had disappeared, and she didn't know what kind of diversion was up his sleeve.

She didn't have to ponder for long because out of nowhere his voice boomed out over the loudspeaker.

"This is the ghost of Candlewick Library. You are trespassers in my house. Leave immediately."

Officer Woolchuck cried out, "Pelican, is that you?"

"No, you fool. I'm over here. And since when do I have a manly voice?"

"I mean no, of course you don't have a masculine…I mean I just was hoping it was you."

"It's the kid, you idiot. He's over the loud speaker. Come on."

They started to run to the front desk of the library, and Boreas's voice echoed through the loud speaker again. "You can run but you can't hide."

Once the coast was clear, Aurora made a running dash, and she didn't stop until she was at the glass window. She banged on it with her fist and tried to make out Otus's shape through the glass. All she saw was the large tree that he had been standing next to but no sign of the giant. She banged on it more forcefully, and then she heard over the loud speaker, "Got you, ghost!"

And then there was screeching feedback as the loudspeaker went dead. Aurora gulped and knew she had to get to the back door. With all her energy, she flew toward the door, not stopping until she got there and fumbled frantically with the door knob. It was locked. She remembered reading something about breaking a lock by using a credit card. Aurora dug her hand into her purse, shuffling the contents wildly until her fingers found her parent's credit card that they gave her in emergencies. This was an emergency. She slid the credit card through the crevice of the door, wiggled it around until finally she was able to pry the lock open. The knob turned and she opened it cautiously. Her eyes screened over the parking lot, making sure that the officers didn't have back-up outside. To her relief, there was only their police car sitting there empty, the red lights on top of the car blinking in a circular motion. She ran as fast as her legs could carry her to the front of the library.

"Otus," Aurora cried out, searching in circles for the giant. He was nowhere to be found. She cried out again, not believing that he had abandoned them. "We need you. It's Aurora. Help us!"

The soft rustling of leaves was all she heard in response. She didn't know what to do. Boreas had been caught by Common Good officers in the library and their giant had run for the hills out of fear. It was up to her to save Boreas, but she had no idea how she could do it.

Aurora crept back toward the officer's vehicle and saw that they had left their keys in the ignition. Instead of talking herself out of it, she quickly opened the driver's side door and slid into the front seat. She had just gotten her learner's permit for driving that year and went through the steps in her head. Check mirrors, put gear into drive. The officer's two-way car radio was crackling with the terrifying voice of Inspector Herald asking for an update.

"Officer Pelican, respond. Did you find the trespassers? Answer me."

Aurora took a deep breath knowing what she was doing was breaking a million laws. She picked up the walkie-talkie and in her most masculine voice responded, "Nabbed the kids. Bringing them to headquarters shortly."

She turned off the walkie-talkie, and the Inspector crackled back, "Good. Bring them to me immediately. We need to make an example of them trespassing during the Sacred Hour."

"Ten-four."

She threw the walkie-talkie back into its holster. Her eyes focused on a button labeled *Siren,* but she hesitated. The Inspector's words haunted her, but she was out of options. She pressed the button and left all hope behind.

Her foot moved from the brake onto the accelerator and started to drive, the siren blaring as she did wheelies in the library parking lot. As she predicted, the two officers came dashing out of the library, tripping over each other. They called out to her to stop, chasing her in the parking lot; Aurora laughed, playing this game with them. The officers were chasing her, but there was no sign of Boreas. He had to be still inside the library. She had hoped they would have taken him out with them, but no such luck.

"Otus, where are you?" she grumbled, exasperated.

She put the car in neutral and opened the front door, rolling out as the car continued heading toward Main Street. She hid behind a hydrangea bush as the officers continued to chase the car down, blaming each other for leaving the keys in the car.

"It was kids. I didn't think they would give us this kind of trouble," Officer Woolchuck stammered, out of breath.

"Shut up and catch the car!" Officer Pelican cried out.

Aurora's knee was bleeding from where she had hit the pavement, but she ignored it and made a running dash for the back door of the library. It was still open, and she ran in. "Boreas, where are you?"

"I'm here," he shouted back. "I'm handcuffed to one of the shelves."

She followed his voice and found him sprawled out on his back on the floor with his left wrist handcuffed to the shelf.

"Aurora, get out of here," he cried out. "It's no good if we are both caught. Where is Otus?"

"Otus is gone," she replied, huffing and puffing as she examined the handcuffs. "Shoot, how are we going to get you out of this?"

"Where are the officers?"

"Chasing a car, but not for long. They'll be headed back here and very angry. We have to get out of here."

"Unless you have a saw or a key in that bag of yours, you need to get out of here."

Aurora searched the front desk of the library for anything that was sharp that could work. She found a paper slicer and shredder but nothing that could cut through the steel handcuffs. She found a hammer and decided to try to break the wooden shelf. She ordered Boreas to sit as far away from the shelf as possible, cleared the books with a sweep of her arm, and heaved with all her strength. The hammer hit the shelf and broke off splinters of wood. She hit it again with all her strength, watching as more of the wood gave way.

"It's working," Boreas cried out, continuing to eye the door for any signs of the officers returning.

She continued to hit the same spot over and over again, remembering her father teaching her when they took apart a bench in their backyard. "Keep hitting the same spot like a bull's eye," he would say. "Then aim and strike. It will break under the force." She struck again and again until finally the shelf collapsed and Boreas was free, the handcuff dangling from his wrist.

"Come on," she shouted, grabbing him by the hand and lifting him to his feet. Together they ran for the back door. They just got outside when they were suddenly grabbed by strong hands that held them aggressively by the chest.

"Good try, kiddies," Officer Woolchuck's voice boomed out maniacally. "But we got you in the end."

"You can't arrest a ghost," Boreas rebuked, but then the officer held out his gun and pointed it directly at his left temple.

"Don't tempt me. You are under arrest. Both of you."

Officer Pelican reached to find handcuffs and faced Aurora against the wall. "No more chasing car tricks, girlie. Now you get to ride in the back seat where you belong."

Facing the wall with the brick heaved against her face, Aurora felt the night getting darker. Earlier that day she had woken up like everyone else and here she was, having trespassed into a library and stolen private property, and a Common Good vehicle. Her parents were going to kill her.

Officer Pelican was fumbling with the handcuffs but finally got them untangled and was about to fasten them on Aurora's wrists when she noticed an obstruction to the moonlight. Her head lurched upward as she let out a high pitched scream, and the handcuffs dropped from her hands, clanging against the cement.

Officer Woolchuck exclaimed, "What on earth is the matter with you, Pelican? This is no time to be afraid of the dark."

He then was lifted off the ground, his squeal even more high pitched than his partner, and his gun plummeted to the ground.

"Put me down!" the officer's voice cried out. "Please don't eat me!"

Boreas and Aurora whirled around to behold Otus lifting the officer into the air. Officer Pelican ran to the car to call for help, but Aurora and Boreas both tackled her simultaneously, and she hit the ground. Aurora picked up the handcuffs and snapped them onto her wrists.

"Listen to me," Aurora said. "We're not going to hurt you."

"What is that thing?" Officer Pelican cried out, her eyes bulging out of her head.

"It will eat you if you don't cooperate," Boreas replied, winking at Aurora. She smiled slightly and then observed Otus still holding onto the other officer, who looked like he was about to pee in his pants.

"Put him down, Otus," she said, nearly laughing. "We'll lock them up in the backseat of the Common Good vehicle so they can't follow us."

Aurora found the handcuff key out of Officer Pelican's pocket and unlocked the latch. Boreas clutched his left wrist gratefully and massaged it to regain blood flow. Aurora used the cuffs on the hands of Officer Woolchuck, who was relieved once his feet were back on the ground. He dashed into the back seat of the car without anyone saying a word. Boreas let the air out of each of the car tires, and Aurora slammed the car door shut, took the keys out of the ignition, and handed them to Otus. Then, like Zeus hurling a lightning bolt, Otus threw the keys as far as he could. The metal streaked across the sky and disappeared into the darkness.

They bid their Common Good officer adversaries farewell and jumped onto Otus's palm. He lifted them up like an elevator to his overalls pocket. The officers watched, mystified, through the back-seat window as the giant took an enormous leap into the air and sped off into the darkness. Before they could blink, he vanished into thin air. The officers stared at each other, contemplating their narrow escape and knowing full well that Inspector Herald was never going to believe their tale about a giant.

Chapter 7

The Handshake

A loud crash of thunder was the prelude to an onslaught of raindrops. Otus screeched to a halt, and Aurora ordered him to help her down from his pocket. His fingers picked her up gently and planted her down on the grass. She recognized that they were in the wooded picnic area of Candlewick Park, where she had come with her parents for a family picnic every summer since she was eight years old. She didn't care to reminisce on those innocent days as she trudged through thick mud up to her ankles. All she wanted to do was go home.

"Where are you going?" Boreas shouted after her.

"Everyone knows the worst place in a thunderstorm is under trees, which is exactly where we're standing right now."

Otus chased Aurora and put his foot out in front of her, but she continued under his legs like a tunnel.

"We can go somewhere else," Otus offered, wiping the rain-drops out of his eyes. A lightning bolt illuminated the sky over his head, and Aurora looked up momentarily but then kept walking. Like playing a game, Otus charged in front of her, blocking her passage of escape.

"What's wrong?" he asked.

She tried to run around him, but he cut her off at every turn, his calf muscles playing the part of walls blocking her escape; it was as if he was dancing the mambo around her.

"I won't let you pass until you answer me."

"Answer him, Aurora," Boreas cried out, turning a shade of green. "Or I'm going to get sick."

Aurora glared up at the gargantuan face nearly hidden by the gray clouds hovering overhead. Another flash of lightning struck nearby, and she wished it had struck his head, being the tallest point in that space.

"You want to know what's wrong? Fine. Where the hell were you, Otus?"

Otus stared back at her, confounded. "I came back."

"Exactly. Came back. Why did you leave us in the first place? Boreas was nearly arrested, and I commandeered a Common Good vehicle. And now they probably have every soldier in the Common Good army looking for us and especially you right now. You are not inconspicuous. You're a giant!"

"Aurora," Boreas whispered, "he did rescue us."

"After the fact! After he was off gallivanting or wherever he was. Now I am a fugitive, and this fugitive wants to get far away from you and your ridiculous mission, and from you too, Boreas. I never want to see either of you again."

The blistering wind stung her face as she made a mad dash past Otus's thick ankle and dodged through the slight gap that had opened up between his feet. The park exit was only a few more feet away, and she ran against the wind, fighting the warm wet pellets exploding against her skin. Her indigo dress was now smeared with mud and unrecognizable from that morning. The block party itself felt like a lifetime ago, and she pictured her bed and her sanctuary away from this madness. She wanted to close herself away from the world again and not let a conch shell drive her away from who she was. She was Fatty Alvarez! That was all she ever was going to be.

She reached the exit and nearly collapsed under the gazebo, catching her breath as the roof took the brunt of the raindrops. She heard Boreas calling out to her, but she ignored him and wished herself invisible under that safety net. No such luck, as Boreas bounded into the gazebo, tracking mud and dripping wet. He took a moment to catch his breath and noticed her huddled in the corner. He kept his eye on her in the event she bounced to her feet and took off again.

"You can't just run away from this," he finally spit out. His fingers combed through his wet black strands, and his intense eyes focused only on her. The rain ricocheted off the wooden beam like a musical symphony overhead.

"He abandoned us, Boreas."

"Because he was scared! Anyone could see that, but he won't admit it! I don't have to be a genius like you to see that."

"Yeah, I know. I'm the big fat genius. That's what you and your brother and Hattie Pearlton and all the other kids say, isn't it?"

"Aurora, that's not what I—"

"Whatever! Our whole circle is messed up. You, me, Otus. Why should we help him?"

"Because we have to." Boreas was pacing the floor, taking giant steps as he walked back and forth like a pendulum.

Aurora sat up and screamed, "No, Boreas. No! We are nothing to each other. Why should we care what happens to him?"

He froze and his face was beat red, veins bulging out of his neck as he stood over her like a towering inferno.

"Because he has had everyone out to get him, misjudge him, scream at him, and all he wants to do is help. That's all he ever wants, but no one will give him a chance because they can't see the real him. They just ignore him or get mad because he's not what they wanted. Not like his brother. Can never be like his brother. Just a stupid failure!"

Boreas kicked the side of the gazebo and stood there, his mind crawling with inner demons as he slowly backed up until he banged against the cold marble. His body slithered downward until he was directly parallel to Aurora, his left leg twitching and he had turned pale, nearly as white as a ghost. The restless rain pitter pattered against the roof like beating drums. Aurora watched uneasily as his face clouded with pain, yet she slid over to his side of the gazebo, slowly and stealthily dragging her bare legs against the floor until she was beside him, his body warm and his chest heaving up and down. She put her head on his shoulder until their breaths were in unison.

"I am sorry," she said, her voice echoed throughout the marble gazebo, the rain slowing down and in rhythm with their heart beats.

He stared down into her eyes and then immediately shifted his weight to the right so that there was a gap between them.

"Yeah, well, you should be apologizing to someone else."

She stood up as she watched him tying his shoelace, his face pointing downward, and he didn't say anything else as she headed toward the Romanesque doorway. She faced outward, smelling the early morning dew, the raindrops glistening on the blades of grass. A hint of sunlight was starting to stream through the gray clouds, fighting to break through and start a new day. It was past the Sacred Hour. They had lived straight through it, and she took a deep breath, welcoming the dawn. It was almost as if her tears had covered the Earth as dew.

"Funny," she said, speaking more to herself than to Boreas. "This time yesterday I didn't believe in giants."

She treaded outwards without daring to look back, not even sure if he had heard her. Nearly halfway through the park she turned around, still feeling Boreas's presence lingering on her skin. She only turned around once to make sure he wasn't still there.

Otus was playing with a tree branch that had been struck by lightning, and when he heard her approaching he turned to face her and offered the tree branch as a peace offering.

"It's still burnt where it got struck. Do you see?" He knelt down onto one knee and held out the branch to her. She took it and observed the singed edge that was still smoking from where it had been struck by electricity and detached from the living organism.

"It just takes a second for your life to change," she said, gazing from the tree branch to Otus, who was fidgeting with his hands now that he didn't have the branch to distract him.

He shook a tree so that green leaves showered down around them. "I thought I needed to run away like I always did before when I saw the red flickering light and the loud siren noise. So I did. But I heard you. I heard you ask for help. And I found my way back. Just a little late."

"I was a little late too, in coming around," she said, taking a deep breath. "I'm so sorry for running off and saying what I said. But I promise, Otus, I won't run off on you again."

She spoke solemnly sitting, like a soaked and tired ragdoll on his knee, but stared up into his eyes with conviction in her words. She was staring into the face of the only person she had ever made a promise to, and it felt right.

"I won't run off on you again either," Otus agreed.

She took his pinky finger and shook it up and down in a hand-shake motion. "This means that we shook on it, that we made a promise to each other."

His rosy pinky fingernail was as large as her entire hand, but this simple gesture caused a bond between human and giant, one that neither had ever experienced before.

Chapter 8

Mrs. Xiomy

Aurora quickly slid the note onto the top of her father's history magazines as she glanced down at her watch. It was nearly the time of the Awakened Hour, and she felt her heart cringe as she glanced around at the pigsty that was her house. Everything was still in its proper place, exactly where she had left it the day before; the magazines still piled high, the beanie babies and stamp collection still towering like the Leaning Tower of Pisa. Soon everyone would be off to work and school, following their early morning routines, listening to the same satellite radio disc jockeys reporting on the weather and traffic jams. Aurora saw her reflection through the microwave glass. The dirt had been showered away, and her indigo dress was on the floor of her room. She'd torn it to shreds since there was no way she was going to be able to unzip herself out of that harness by herself. She was now more comfortably dressed in jeans and a black short-sleeved shirt with her horoscope sign embroidered on the front in pink stitches. She was an Aquarius and bore the symbol of the water bearer. She always thought it was ironic that her sign was bearing water, though the element was air. Two squiggly lowercase M's were depicted on the cotton fabric of her shirt.

The Common Good approved of astrology and had voted that it was more on the same line as psychology, giving the people an inside glance at themselves and the inner workings of their person-ality. The stars were balls of gas and had been proven as such. They were not molded by the hands of a god or goddess, spinning them through the atmosphere and dictating a human's life through a crys-tal ball.

Otus was hiding in the Candlewick Park cave, which was right on the coastline of the south shore where the waves from the Atlantic Ocean crashed their foamy hands against the solid brown rock that had formed after thousands of years of erosion. This cave was closed off to park dwellers due to some kids being found smok-ing in the dwelling. To prevent trespassers, a large sturdy wooden plank had been built to completely cover and seal the mouth of the cave. It hadn't anticipated a giant. In one fluid motion, Otus ripped the wooden door off its hinges and managed to keep the barrier intact but allow passage for them to enter the hiding place. They had asked Otus to replace the barrier while they were away. When they returned, the teenagers would knock on it three times. Boreas had told him that if someone else tried to enter then Otus was to eat them.

"I don't eat people," Otus replied, horrified. "I'm not a cannibal."

"Oh, I guess I watched too much *Jack and the Beanstalk* growing up," Boreas laughed. He instead instructed Otus to impersonate a ghost and holler so loud that its sound would reverberate off its hollow walls and sound so frightening that the trespassers would flee for their life. The cave's notorious legend of being haunted would help in that matter too.

Aurora closed the door to her house quietly behind her, careful to not awaken her parents. Once they received her letter they wouldn't be so worried. She doubted her parents would believe the story she made up about going to try to find Mary Fray in Iowa, but at least they could rationalize it once they saw wanted pictures of herself around town (five of which she had noticed on her way back to Wishbone Avenue). She flung her backpack over her shoulder, having packed some necessities; extra pairs of underwear, clothes, sweatshirt, gloves, boots, flashlight and some food provisions that she had borrowed from her parent's pantry. If they were to travel toward the northern lights, she couldn't dress in only t-shirts and tank tops.

Boreas was sitting on the curb at the corner stop sign, and she stopped short for a second, remembering when she would meet Mary at this same spot so many times before school. This same corner stop sign was where they had shared so many fun memories. Aurora stood looking at that red octagonal stop sign and wished she had known Otus earlier. Then maybe they could have saved Mary. Now she was somewhere in Iowa or wherever the Inspector had forced her and her family to go. She pictured Mary's owl eyes smiling at Aurora and knew that Mary would be proud that Aurora was chosen for this quest. Mary would know she was doing what she thought was right, and doing what was right was helping Otus.

Boreas stood up. He had also showered and changed into a blue t-shirt, black jeans and a large brimmed newsy styled peddler hat. He was stepping on a used firecracker with the balls of his foot as he noticed Aurora approaching.

"What took you so long? I had to dodge two Common Good vehicles coming down the avenue. I think they are doing a barricade up by the library. Did you leave a note?"

She nodded, looking back at her house where her parents were still sleeping soundly, unaware that their daughter wouldn't be home once they awakened.

"Yeah. You?"

"They won't even know I'm missing."

Aurora shook her head at Boreas. "You don't mean that."

"You should know that my relationship with my father is not the greatest," Boreas snickered. "You heard our father-son talk yesterday at the barbeque."

Aurora bit her lip. He had not forgotten that she had eavesdropped on their conversation when his father was berating him about the burned hamburgers.

"Ever since my mom died when I was five he has never treated me the same. Everything is about Jonathan, who can do no wrong. I'm just an afterthought to him, a failure to the family name."

He kicked the used firecracker so that it went flying to the other side of the street.

"Boreas," Aurora sat down on the curb and tied her shoe for the tenth time, "why did you quit the tennis team before the playoffs?"

Boreas swung his backpack over his right shoulder and muttered, "Why do you care?"

"You were the best player on the team. If you had something to prove to your father, why quit?"

He stuffed his hands into his pockets and said, "I quit when I realized I have nothing to prove to my father. I shouldn't have to prove anything to him or anyone in that stupid school. But they all expect me to be something or someone I'm not. So I ran away from home, and that was when I got caught outside during the Sacred Hour."

She took a deep breath and looked down Wishbone Avenue at the brimstone cottage that had been the Fray residence. She remembered that Mary wanted to know how Boreas got out of Candlewick Prison alive.

"How did you do it?"

He fixed his backpack, half-listening. "How did I do what?"

"How did you escape from Candlewick Prison?"

Boreas looked at her curiously, and then the cold front that he had mastered for so many years melted from the corners of his eyes.

"Inspector Herald can't win all the time, Aurora." He dug into his pocket, pulled out a pair of sunglasses, and smiled mischievously as he put them on. "Now come on. We have to coerce Mrs. Xiomy to come with us to meet Otus at the caves. And we'll need more than my charm to convince her."

"This is not going to be easy," she thought as they raced down to the cul-de-sac at the end of Wishbone Avenue.

✲ ✲ ✲

Mrs. Xiomy lived in a Victorian-style house that was surrounded by indigo and orange rhododendron bushes that blocked the house from view on the street. Monstrous weeping willow trees drooped down and danced wistfully to the sound of Tchaikovsky, which was blasting from the first floor window. The ballerina-like movements caused Aurora and Boreas to dance around their entangling tresses. The front yard resembled an ostentatious botanical garden, with every plant and flower labeled with its Latin origin nomenclature. There was the *Leucospermum nutans*, which resembled pink jellyfish tentacles on a stem, and another read *Phalaenopsis amabilis,* or butterfly orchids, which were ivory in color and blended in with the white snowball hydrangea bushes. Though inviting in color and flowers, the giant "X" on the door foretold all visitors to beware.

"If I didn't know a beautiful teacher lived here, I would say this is the home of the witch from Hansel and Gretel," Boreas mumbled under his breath.

Aurora grabbed hold of the brass horseshoe shaped door knocker and banged it twice against the door. The Tchaikovsky waltz continued to blast throughout the house, and they pressed their ears directly against the door to try to make out any footprints or voices. None were heard as the waltz continued to crescendo for the grand finale.

"Maybe she's not home."

"Maybe we should come back later."

As they were speaking out loud, the door heaved open, lurching their bodies forward, and they landed on their sides on a pasty white rug. A woman's figure stood between them.

"Aurora! Boreas! What on earth are you doing here?"

They picked themselves up off the rug and were face to face with Mrs. Xiomy. Her golden hair was braided and tied back in a low bun, and she wore thin purple glasses that covered her amethyst eyes.

"Hi, Mrs. Xiomy," Aurora blurted out. The waltz was skipping, and the same four notes were playing over and over again in an eerie pattern and Mrs. Xiomy quickly walked over to a phonograph machine, where she scratched the needle off the vinyl record.

"Is that a record machine?" Aurora asked, eyeing the contraption that she had only heard her father speak of.

"Shouldn't you both be headed to class?" she asked suspiciously, eyeing the two visitors while proceeding to tidy up the room. A big chow dog with a bear face, little ears, and a thick coat of fur came dashing into the room and started licking Boreas, who was knocked onto the floor by the furry brown pet. The dog licked him over and over again on the cheek and Boreas's peddler hat nearly flew off his head.

"Newton, get down," Mrs. Xiomy commanded. She put her lips together and blew a high pitched whistle. Boreas seemed fascinated by her red lips when she puckered them together. Aurora grabbed him and yanked on his arm until he was on his feet.

"Sorry about that. He has a mind of his own. Don't you, Newton baby?" She rustled his tousled hair.

"Um, we're not going to class today, Mrs. Xiomy," Aurora said, hating herself for having rehearsed this in her head the entire walk over and then forgetting everything.

"Why? Are you ill? If it's contagious get out quick so that I can disinfect. Newton is susceptible to germs. But you both look healthy. A bit out of sorts, perhaps. But then again, it's not often that I get visitors."

"I'd love to visit you anytime you'd like," Boreas exclaimed heartily, and Aurora elbowed him violently in the chest.

"I can make you some tea. You both are early birds this morning."

They followed Mrs. Xiomy into her kitchen, which was wedding white and so pristine that Aurora could see her reflection in the tiled floor. The teacher put some water in the tea kettle and ignited the stove.

"I didn't realize that you were friends."

"Oh, we're not really," Boreas said hurriedly.

"I mean, we just really talked for the first time yesterday," Aurora added, finding it difficult to get comfortable on the wooden stool where the seat consisted of geological rocks digging into her behind.

Mrs. Xiomy adjusted her glasses on the edge of her pointed nose and got out two mugs and teabags. "I know what this is about."

Boreas and Aurora stared at each other hurriedly. "You do?"

She sat down and set the mugs in front of the two teenagers. "I mean there's nothing to worry about. This happens to people your age and I am glad that you trusted me enough to come to me during this time. There are options that we can explore together, and I can be there when you tell your parents."

"Excuse me?" Aurora's words stumbled out of her mouth.

"It's a difficult decision, especially when you are not married… but a baby can change your life, not that I would know, but from what I've heard."

"Wait, wait," Aurora interrupted her teacher. "Do you think I'm pregnant?"

Mrs. Xiomy stared back at her, "I mean, it's nothing to be ashamed about."

Aurora felt her blood boil and stood up abruptly, "I knew this was a mistake."

Boreas was falling over from laughter as the tea kettle erupted with an earsplitting whistle. Mrs. Xiomy jumped up and turned it off hurriedly.

"I am sorry, but I think that I am confused. I just thought that you two were here together and before class…"

"I didn't knock her up," Boreas said, nearly hiccupping. "I mean, unless there's another father, Aurora?"

She gave him a dirty look and resumed her seat on the bench, readjusting her butt so that it was more comfortable.

Mrs. Aurora was red in the face as she poured the tea water and handed the mugs to the teenagers. "I apologize that I jumped the gun. So let's please start over. What can I help you both with?"

Aurora took a sip of her tea, and the steam resonated on her face as she gathered her courage. "We just were curious—well, more than curious—and it's for a project of sorts that we are working on together and need information about…do you know anything about something called a Geometric Storm?"

"Eloquently put," Boreas mumbled, his voice echoing through the tea mug.

"A Geometric Storm? What class is this for?"

"Um, our math class."

"Mr. Strident shouldn't be teaching anything about astronomy. I will speak with him once I get to the classroom. Now you can forget this project because I am going to give him a piece of my mind before the principal finds out."

"So wait, do you know what this storm is?" Boreas quickly interjected.

"Of course I know what it is, but the Geometric Storm is not on the mandated curriculum set for us by the Common Good government. Mr. Strident is trying to get himself and the rest of the faculty into trouble, and I am not going to deal with the Inspector. Not for something like this!"

She stood up, grabbed her peanut-shaped purse off the counter, and flung it over her shoulder.

"Mrs. Xiomy, we're not being honest with you," Aurora exclaimed, feeling the truth was the only way they were going to pry this information out of their teacher. "There is no project. Well, no school project for that matter. Boreas and I are helping someone get to the northern lights. He says he needs to get there when the Geometric Storm hits, but we don't know anything else—what this storm is, when it is coming, and the exact coordinates we need to get to. Are you able to help us?"

Mrs. Xiomy dropped her purse onto the countertop, and it ricocheted off the tiled floor with a tremendous bang. Her face turned as white as the kitchen counter.

"It's impossible," she gasped.

"What is impossible?" Aurora pried, standing up and facing her teacher.

Mrs. Xiomy's eyes bulged wide. She removed her glasses and flung them down to her side. She continued to stare at them, from one to the next, her eyes growing wider and wider. Her finger pointed from one to the other as if she were in a hypnotic trance.

"Aurora Borealis," she whispered. Before Aurora could say anything, Mrs. Xiomy fell straight backward. Boreas dove and caught her head before it banged against the tiled floor. She had passed out, her eyes rolling to the back of her head.

"She fainted!" Aurora exclaimed, running to grab a cold compress and water.

Boreas lifted her to the couch, and they put her head against a pillow. Aurora draped the cold compress on her forehead and lifted her legs onto the ledge of the couch to get blood circulating to her brain.

"Well, that went well," Boreas said, fanning her face. "Now our names cause teachers to faint. What is going to happen next?"

Aurora shrugged and checked her pulse. Mrs. Xiomy finally came around and opened her eyes as the color returned to her face. She shrieked slightly when seeing the youths, but Aurora quickly reassured her that she was okay and had fainted. Her head did not hit the floor, and there was no need to rush to the hospital. She just needed to rest until she felt better.

"Aurora Borealis," she repeated, staring from one face to the other. "This is impossible. I am going mad. Yes, I am mad."

"Maybe all of us are mad," Boreas agreed, patting a pillow for the teacher who was weighing the situation.

"Get out of my house! Both of you! Conspirators! Are you spies of the Common Good?"

Aurora reached into her backpack and pulled out the article that she had stolen from the library with Mrs. Xiomy's picture on it. "We are not against you. We think you are someone who can help us!"

She thrust the picture into her hands, and Mrs. Xiomy stared at it, not comprehending how this article was discovered. She methodically traced the outline of the man being led away by the authorities with her finger.

"He was your husband, wasn't he?"

Mrs. Xiomy nodded solemnly. "Yes, he was my husband." She crumpled the photograph in her clutch and unraveled her scarf from around her neck. Like a lioness attacking her prey, she wrapped the silk scarf around Boreas's neck and started choking him with all her force, strangling him.

"Who are you working for? Who are you helping? Tell me or I swear I'll kill him."

Boreas was gagging for breath, and Aurora quickly tried to grab the scarf, but Mrs. Xiomy instead pulled on it tighter, causing Boreas to gag for breath, falling to his knees. Aurora stood there helpless as her teacher held all the cards with a maniacal glow shining in her eyes. She clutched her hands tighter around his neck, and Boreas reached out for help, but his arms collapsed hanging nearly lifeless at his side.

"Answer me, Aurora, or he dies!"

Aurora cried out, "Otus. His name is Otus."

"Who or what is Otus?"

"Please stop it! You're killing him."

"Who is he?"

She turned from Boreas back to her teacher and then back to Boreas again. His eyes pleaded to not give up the information, but she couldn't help it. They were in this together, whether he liked it or not.

She blurted out, "A giant. He's a giant."

Mrs. Xiomy released her hold on Boreas, and pushed him to the ground. Aurora ran to his side and quickly unraveled the scarf from around his neck. She checked to make sure he was okay, but he pushed her away from him as his lungs were filling with air once again.

"She's crazy," Boreas stammered, getting to his feet and holding onto Aurora for support.

Mrs. Xiomy rose, knocking all the pillows off the couch, and marched over to her where the phonograph was sitting. She put her hands down on the mantelpiece and started murmuring to herself, "You were right, David! I can't believe you were right after all this time."

Aurora still held Boreas by his arm and eyed the door. They started inching their way toward it, and she said fearfully, "Look, we're just going to leave now, okay? Please just forget everything we said."

Mrs. Xiomy turned toward the two teenagers, and her maniacal face had transformed into one of congeniality. "Please take a seat. I'll be just a minute. Need to pull a book from the library."

They both obediently sat back down onto the couch, staring at this now angelic woman standing before them.

"I never thought I'd say this, but I'm terrified of this woman," Boreas whispered, and Aurora nodded, clenching her teeth and trying to think how they were going to get out of this mess. Otus was still in the caves waiting for them and most likely wondering what was taking them so long. It wasn't like it was nighttime when he was able to roam freely. During the day he was bound to cause a panic throughout Candlewick.

Mrs. Xiomy removed the record and then pressed a button on the machine. Instantly the wood paneling on the staircase gave way to reveal a large bookshelf lined with books. Aurora's mouth opened wide in shock at this secret hiding spot. Mrs. Xiomy was whistling and pulling books off the shelf, and finally Aurora was done being afraid. She stood up with the silk scarf wrapped around her wrist.

"Look, are you going to help us or not? Because if you dare attack me or Boreas again, we will take you down together. There are wanted posters of us plastered all over town so don't think that we have anything to lose. And at this point my parents have read my letter and think either I've gone crazy or that I am eloping right now. So don't piss me off again!"

Mrs. Xiomy sat down on the pink sofa and applauded Aurora. She replaced her purple glasses onto her nose but couldn't hide the stoic expression on her face. "You've got courage yet, Aurora. Good. You're going to need it, both of you, if you are going to help your giant. Because the Common Good will kill you before you have a chance to. Mark my words for that. They have no problem with sacrificing two little teenagers in order to save the world as they know it. That's what we've all been taught. The greater good is for the common good. That is the message drilled into our brains since the Last Straw Protest failed."

She bent down and picked up the crumpled piece of newspaper. She smoothed it out until there was hardly a wrinkle over the man's face.

"This is the only picture that was ever taken of him. In fact, I didn't know that this picture still existed. I was so young then. A little older than the two of you. Protesting with my husband David Xiomy, better known as IMAM.

"You kids found out about my past life. Yes, I was a protestor against the Common Good and was a part of the religious protestors. I was in the Last Straw protest in which fifteen people were killed and forty people arrested, including myself and David. I was tortured, and to spare my husband's life, I gave away crucial information about the revolution that ultimately lead to its demise. And Inspector Herald repaid me handsomely. He went back on every word he promised and ended up executing my husband anyway. Told the media that it was for everyone's benefit that he not live while this world thrived.

"But there was a loophole in that plan. Before David died, there was a professor who was administering a new scientific drug to torture him. This professor eventually grew to admire David, like so many did, and was the last person to see him alive. David told him to spread the word to me and to others like me. He spoke about a Geometric Storm. The professor thought he was confusing it with the geological storm, space disturbances, or explosions that cause electrical outages on Earth close to the polar caps. But my husband was insistent. He told the professor to find me and together to find this book that would speak about a Geometric Storm that would cause massive destruction and loss of human lives throughout the country. He said that the book also tells of a force that could prevent massive pandemonium, a spiritual force of a giant amongst men. This giant will be able to prevent this catastrophe. That he will be at the Aurora Borealis and, sided with the chosen two bearing the same name, together they will uncover the balance of equilibrium and save the Earth from destruction. The past and the future tied together hand in hand."

"Where is this book?" Boreas exclaimed, sitting on the edge of the seat.

"There is no book. At least I never found it. If such a book did exist, the Common Good has destroyed all traces of it."

"Maybe the professor has it?"

"The professor died ten years ago. Along with your mother, Boreas. The two of them, along with many others, died in the Candlewick Prison burning. They were friends, the professor and your mother."

"Did you know my mother?" Boreas asked slowly.

Mrs. Xiomy nodded. "Yes, I knew Fawn Stockington. She was my best friend, until…"

"Until what?"

She closed her eyes as if reminiscing on a painful memory but snapped out of it, saying, "It's not important. What is important is that both of you, sharing the same name of Aurora Borealis and speaking of a giant…it just makes me wonder if there was some truth in the prophecy my husband foretold."

The three of them sat staring at each other, taking in this information of a prophecy that was coming true.

"We need to speak to Otus." Aurora stood up resolutely. "He knew about the Geometric Storm. Maybe he knows about this book too."

"Otus? You mean the giant?" Mrs. Xiomy asked, enthralled.

Boreas grabbed Aurora to the side. "Do you think this is a good idea? I mean the woman is positively nuts. I mean she tried to kill me!"

"Oh yeah, and you're welcome, by the way."

"For what? Standing there like a paraplegic as she tried to suck the life out of me?"

"Whatever. Next time I won't be so generous. I'll let whoever it is suck the life out of you and stand by and urge them to finish you off, you ungrateful runt."

He laughed uncontrollably. "Now I'm a runt. This is getting better and better. Stuck with two women. Thank God Otus is a guy or I'd jump off a cliff and save the Common Good a load of trouble."

Mrs. Xiomy pulled open the garage door. She had a purple Fiat smart car that could sit only two people comfortably. Aurora recalled reading about these small compact cars. She had never seen one up close before and turned to her teacher, concerned.

"Mrs. Xiomy, are we all riding in that car?"

"You two need to squeeze in the front seat, and I'm going to cover you with Newton."

She pulled the passenger seat as far back as it could go, which left about six feet for them to cram into.

"I think this is physically impossible," Boreas protested, examining the car. "I don't think that your dog could fit in that car, let alone three of us."

"Well, it's either that, my young friends, or you walk, and at this hour Wishbone Avenue is going to be crawling with the Common Good officials who you said are in hot pursuit of you and your giant friend Otus. I think I would prefer squeezing into a smart car than into one of their vehicles. Newton!"

She whistled, and Newton came bumbling toward her. He sat waiting for Boreas and Aurora to make the first move.

Boreas smiled, "After you."

Aurora shook her head. "No, by all means. You go first."

Mrs. Xiomy opened the door and exclaimed, "I'll push you both in and make Newton pee on you if you don't get into that vehicle in the next ten seconds."

Boreas reluctantly made the first move, probably more out of fear of Mrs. Xiomy than out of being a chivalrous gentleman. He crouched down onto the floor of the smart car until he couldn't scrunch any more. Aurora sat nearly on top of him as she maneuvered her way into the car. Mrs. Xiomy the whole time was relaying a story of how nineteen teenage women were able to fit into one of these cars at one point in time. Aurora looked around and didn't think that was physically possible.

Newton jumped onto the passenger seat, and Aurora hoped that he would sit still and not squish them, which really would cause her to hyperventilate. Mrs. Xiomy, as a finishing touch to her masterpiece and gushing at her brilliant idea, threw a blanket over the two teenagers, just in case they got stopped on their way to the Candlewick Park.

"Can't take any chances," she beamed, turning the key. The little Fiat roared to life and maneuvered its way down the manicured driveway.

Boreas kept trying to shift, saying that his foot was falling asleep. Aurora tried shifting her weight but then he complained that his other foot was falling asleep. Getting aggravated, she put all of her weight on both of his legs so that he would shut up. They headed down Wishbone Avenue and hit a huge bump, which resulted in Boreas hitting his head against the glove compartment and Aurora nearly flying directly into the passenger seat. Her head was cushioned by the soft fur of Newton, who barked a "you're welcome" in dog language. It seemed like an eternity, and Aurora felt as if her body would be stuck in that position forever, clamped to Boreas's knees and having to be stuck to him like Siamese twins when Boreas took her hand and gave it a gentle squeeze. Aurora looked at him quizzically, but he murmured that he needed to remind himself that he still had feeling in his body. Aurora squeezed it back, but her hand was clammy, so she quickly pulled it away.

The car swerved down Wishbone Avenue, and Mrs. Xiomy said that there was a police car parked in front of both the Alvarez and the Stockington residences. All the neighbors were out of their houses, congregating around the driveways to get news about what happened. Mrs. Xiomy turned on the radio, and Aurora and Boreas perked up their ears to listen to the announcer.

"At the cusp of the Sacred Hour, two teenagers, now identified as Aurora Alvarez and Boreas Stockington, were found trespassing in the Candlewick Private National Library. They attacked two Common Good officers and stole one book. I repeat, one book has been stolen and an article ripped out of the Archives. Stockington and Alvarez are fugitives of the state. If you have any information about their whereabouts please call your local precinct immediately. It is for the Common Good that they be caught. The IDEAL has spoken."

Mrs. Xiomy looked down and smiled at the teenagers. "You two were busier than you let on. I am so proud to be your teacher."

Aurora breathed a sigh of relief. At least the announcement hadn't mentioned a thirty-foot-tall giant. Officers Woolchuck and Pelican were either too embarrassed to admit it, or they had only told their superiors, who wanted to keep that part hushed up to the public.

Just then she heard a scream from outside the car, and she felt her blood run cold. It was her mother's scream. She quickly removed the blanket covering her and stole a glance out the window. There was her mother, looking disheveled and wearing only her red bathrobe. She never went out in public without her makeup and her hair perfectly done. And then beside her was her father, Mr. Alvarez, speaking to Inspector Herald, who was ordering another officer to handcuff him. Her father's face was strong and steady, and she saw the Inspector strike him across the cheek with a copy of his *History* magazine. The paper sliced his cheek, and blood oozed out. She couldn't watch anymore, and before Mrs. Xiomy could stop her, she flung open the door and rolled out, hitting the pavement hard against her chest. She heard Boreas cry out to her, but she didn't listen. She got to her feet and screamed out, "Dad!"

He looked up, the blood dripping down his face. Mrs. Alvarez ran up to her daughter and threw her arms around her. "Aurora, tell me this isn't true! Tell me this isn't true."

Aurora couldn't answer and felt her eyes glazed with tears as she turned and looked into the notorious face of Inspector Herald. He smiled, licking the tip of his front chipped tooth in satisfaction. He stood six foot seven inches in height, and was dressed formally in the Common Good uniform except for the long black trench coat that covered the length of his body. His right sleeve bore the symbol of the country's flag and the INSPECTOR in bold orange letters. His face was scarred from the infamous Candlewick Prison fire ten years earlier, and he attempted to cover it with a massive amount of makeup. His bald scalp was covered with a gray fedora, and he stared at Aurora with his piercing coal-black eyes. "Well, Miss Alvarez, so nice of you to join us this morning. And I see that you aren't alone. Guards seize the two in the Fiat. I believe if I am not mistaken that you will find Boreas Stockington and Mrs. Rana Xiomy. Bring them to the Candlewick Prison along with our prestigious guest here."

"What about my father?" Aurora exclaimed.

With a slight grimace, the Inspector ordered the guards to remove the handcuffs from Mr. Alvarez's wrists. "Burn everything in the home. This will set an example to others who have illegal USA nationalistic merchandise. The IDEAL expressly forbids it."

"These were confiscated from other homes, from my own clients," Mr. Alvarez said strongly without any hint of regret. "I was housing them to be destroyed following the Independence Day of the Last Straw. I didn't deem it appropriate to burn on a national holiday, don't you agree?"

Inspector Herald gleamed with delight at this display of wits. "You were right in assuming that, and I will give you until the end of today to see that all of this is burned immediately in your front yard. I will want media coverage of the event to be aired all day and night for the remainder of the week. We have to set an example for other families who might be housing this type of merchandise. I will instruct the Common Good officers to invade each home to ensure the safety of the United States of the Common Good's people from instigators."

"Herald," Mrs. Xiomy screamed out. "You leave these kids alone. They didn't do anything."

Herald walked up to Mrs. Xiomy, touched one of her strands of hair, and said, "Rana, you are as beautiful as ever. Too bad David isn't here to appreciate it."

She spit into his face. The Inspector laughed and wiped the saliva from his eye with his red handkerchief.

"And I see you haven't lost your spirit, even after your loss. Take them out of my sight."

Officer Pelican seized Aurora and quickly handcuffed her, whispering in her ear, "I guess you don't have your giant friend to help you out of this one."

Aurora bit her lip as she turned around and saw Boreas and Mrs. Xiomy being handcuffed and led into another Common Good vehicle. She stole one last glance at her parents, who were huddled together and watching her, looking both worried and frightened. She heard her father's voice call out that she was going to be okay, that he would defend her. She couldn't even cry out to them as the car door slammed shut and locked her inside the back seat of the vehicle. As she rode in shame toward the Candlewick Prison, she saw every face on Wishbone Avenue staring back at her through the clear glass window. She saw each of their faces accusingly glare at her, judging her, even though they didn't know her side of the story. She was the enemy here. She was the one to disappear.

Chapter 9

Candlewick Prison

Candlewick Prison was a fortress, a large, circular structure made of iron with the highest security systems in the world meant to keep their prisoners in and the world out. Nobody had ever seen any media coverage of the prisoners' trials or their executions. The only one seen by the masses had been the public execution of David Xiomy by the hand of Inspector Herald.

Officers Woolchuck and Pelican roughly led Aurora, Boreas, and Mrs. Xiomy into an elevator and then down into the deep sepulcher. It was dank and cold as they walked down a long narrow corridor lined with tiny cells, and it smelled of urine and feces. Putrid yellow fluorescent lights flickered madly above them, and Aurora felt dizzy as she followed the footsteps before her. They passed cell after cell filled with prisoners, each in a cadaverous state, and Aurora recognized the emaciated face of Joshua from

Joshua's Laundromat who had disappeared one week earlier. His hollow eyes followed her as she walked past, and Aurora felt both appalled and frightened.

They were thrown into an empty cell, most likely a transitional until they were tried and pronounced with sentence. As the cell door slammed shut, Aurora immediately felt the severity of the situation sink in.

Mrs. Xiomy paced back and forth examining the stone walls of the prison cell. "I told you to stay still and be quiet. What part of that didn't you understand?"

Aurora slumped down onto the floor, her hand about to reach out to the prison bars but Boreas smacked it away. "It will electrocute you. Believe me, I know."

Aurora quickly pulled her hand back. "I am so sorry. I know you both must hate me, but I couldn't let my parents take the fall for me. I just couldn't."

"So you instead have us take the fall with you," Boreas remarked severely. "Next time can you please warn me of your impromptu kindness? Because it seems to be benefitting everyone except me!"

"Blaming me is not going to get us out of here," Aurora cried out.

"Get out of here?" Mrs. Xiomy laughed deliriously. "Aurora, there is no getting out of here. We are prisoners for life. You think Inspector Herald is going to let you go free, especially now that he knows who you are? He may not be a genius, but I think he can figure out that you are the two from the prophecy. He is going to use you now to get to your giant, if he even exists. And me, well, he is never going to let me see the light of day again, I assure you."

Aurora's mind was whirling in a million directions. She ran over to Boreas. "I think this is a good time for you to tell us how you escaped from here. You have to tell us the truth."

Boreas looked up at her, fear ensconced in his eyes. "You want the truth? The truth is—"

A loud buzzer sounded and interrupted their conversation. Footsteps echoed from the corridor, and Aurora felt the tension in the cell heighten. She feared it would be the Inspector but was hopeful it could be her father come to release them. She was not expecting the face of Jonathan Stockington on the opposite side of that prison cell.

He stood there, his blond hair tied in a ponytail and his big turquoise eyes staring intently back at them. His eyes moved from hers to Mrs. Xiomy until they finally settled on Boreas, who was just as surprised to see him as Aurora was. She felt so humiliated that he was there seeing her in the lowest point of her life. She tried to fix her hair but realized there was no point. He wasn't here in the depths of Candlewick Prison to see her.

Boreas finally called out, "What are you doing here, Jonathan?"

"Dad sent me," Jonathan replied coldly. "He wants you to know that he is not able to save you this time. He warned you that if you got into trouble again his hands would be tied. Inspector Herald did him a favor the last time you violated the Sacred Hour. He cannot intervene again."

Aurora's head swerved to look at Boreas, who sat there with his mouth open in exasperation. Aurora couldn't believe her ears. Boreas had never escaped. His father had gotten permission to let him go free. And all this time she had been fooled like so many others. And he had let them revel in this mystery like he was some great magician.

"Is that all?" Boreas asked, unfazed by the news. "I thought you would bring me a fruit basket as well."

"This is no time for jokes," Jonathan cried out. "This is by far the biggest screw-up you have ever made. And to get Aurora mixed up in this too. I can't believe you would be so selfish."

"He didn't. I mean, we both got into this together," Aurora retorted, finding the words.

"You are defending him?" Jonathan asked accusingly, and then his eyes softened and he called out to the guard, "I want to speak with Miss Alvarez alone if that's possible."

"Yes, Mr. Stockington," the guard answered, putting in the code and dismantling the electric current as the prison bars slid open.

"What do you have to say to her that you can't say to my face?" Boreas growled.

Jonathan shook his head at his younger brother. The guard led Aurora out of the cell and into a private room, where both she and Jonathan were to be together alone. The guard said that they had five minutes, and then the door locked shut behind him.

Jonathan looked genuinely upset as he sat down in a chair and offered her the other facing him.

"Aurora, I am pleading with you. You need to talk some sense into Boreas. He won't listen to me. Maybe he will listen to you. He needs to come clean about the whole thing. If not, I don't know what will happen to him. This is a second offense. It could lead to death."

Aurora felt so vulnerable in Jonathan's presence, staring down at her wrists, still sore where she had been handcuffed. "I don't know what I can do."

"It's the same story. He is always trying to get Dad's attention. Ever since Mom died he has gone down the wrong path, and he envies me. It's obvious. And yes, I know that I am my father's favorite, but do you see me getting locked up in Candlewick Prison? It's like that spring formal when Boreas made a fool of himself singing and I had to beat him up to get the microphone back to the DJ. He won't learn unless it's beaten out of him. I need you to beat the truth out of him. Both of your lives depend on it."

"I don't understand," Aurora said slowly. "What do you want me to find out?"

Jonathan leaned closer toward her, so close to her proximity that she could smell the almond scent of his aftershave lotion.

"Inspector Herald believes he is hiding something. Something detrimental to the security of the country. He needs the whereabouts of this weapon. Do you know about this? Has he told you about this?"

Aurora recoiled back into her chair. She couldn't believe that she had been misled to think that Jonathan cared. Disheartened, she exclaimed, "So I see the Inspector is having you do the dirty work for him!"

"I am trying to save my brother's life! I think you know how far someone would go to save their family." He put his hand on top of hers and Aurora's heart fluttered as his eyes were gazing into hers. "You're smart, Aurora. You'll do the right thing."

Aurora felt hypnotized staring into her crush's eyes and she wanted to tell him that she would help, that she would reveal the whereabouts of this weapon.

The door unlocked, and the guard announced that the five minutes were up. Aurora snapped out of the spell as Jonathan released his hand from her grasp. She stole one last glance at him as the guard led her back into the prison cell, his words still replaying in her mind. The prison bars slammed shut behind her, and she beheld Boreas sitting in a corner, his arms crossed and his hair hanging slightly over his left eye.

"So what did my brother have to say?" he angrily snapped.

"He wants to know the whereabouts of a weapon of national security. They want to know about Otus. And Jonathan says that your life depends on it."

✵ ✵ ✵

Time bore no meaning in the cold, dark depths of Candlewick Prison. There were no windows so the hours wore on, and there was no way to determine if the sun rose or set. The only lights were the flickering fluorescents that seeped through the bars of the prison cell and the little red flickering light of the camera that was omnipresent in the corner. Aurora began to dread that Otus was getting worried waiting for them at the Candlewick Park cave. She feared he would come searching for them and risk getting captured by Inspector Herald and the Common Good army. So far the three of them were the only ones who knew about his whereabouts, but she didn't want to think about the interrogation skills of the Inspector. Mrs. Xiomy had gone into a catatonic state and was busy rocking back and forth in a corner of the prison cell. It was bringing back memories of her last time she had inhabited one of these cells fifteen years before when she had been tortured and had given up key information to try to save her husband's life.

"The Inspector cannot be trusted," she repeated over and over again in her rambling state. Boreas was busy pacing back and forth trying to not go crazy. Aurora listened to the sounds of the wailing and crying from the corridor where so many like herself were imprisoned.

"How long have they kept us in the dark?" she thought solemnly. "It's almost as if we wanted to be ignorant and pretend that everything was okay."

She started thinking that maybe Mary was down here in these dungeons, not in Iowa like the media had claimed. After seeing Joshua from Joshua's Laundromat, she began to think the others who had disappeared from their town of Candlewick were down here too. Perhaps they had been down here all this time. Why hadn't her father ever told her? Why did he lie to her and say everyone got a fair trial and was given equal rights?

"He probably wanted to protect you," Boreas had replied after she had vented to him. "And if he had told you the truth, would you have believed him?"

"I don't know," she said slowly. "I wanted to believe that Mary had been taken to Iowa. If I knew she was down here this whole time, I would never have forgiven myself. And now we might never get out of here."

She felt so scared and alone that the tears started falling. Boreas wrapped his arms around her, and she cried into his shoulder.

"We are not going to die down here," he said reassuringly. "We will find a way out."

They had not been given any food or water since they had arrived, and Aurora felt stomach pangs as she tried to stay awake. She heard a sound outside the prison, thinking it was someone bringing them food, but instead she smelled the sweet aromas of chicken soup passing them and going to the neighboring cell.

"They are going to make us starve to death!" she wailed.

Mrs. Xiomy shook her head at the young girl, saying, "They won't kill you yet. Not until they get what they want out of you."

An empty bowl of soup was thrown into their cell, and Boreas and Aurora both lunged for it, but it had been licked clean. A pit of emptiness overwhelmed her as Aurora looked up to behold two eyes staring at her through the bars. She knew that they were in trouble now as he started to punch in the numeric code and the bars slid to the side. He stood up over them like a towering shadow and pointed his gun at them. Behind him were two armed guards who stood anchored at a standstill in the doorway.

Mrs. Xiomy struggled to her feet and ushered Aurora and Boreas to do the same.

"He's the First Lieutenant." The words came out of her mouth like she was choking on her own fear.

Famished and dehydrated, Aurora walked in a haze down the corridor and was pushed into a small white cell that smelled of mildew. The table inside was stained with dry blood. Aurora felt sick as the door closed shut behind her. She cried out to Mrs. Xiomy and Boreas, but only silence echoed back. She had been separated from her friends, and she knew this was part of their interrogation ploy. She stood there immobilized and helpless as the First Lieutenant took a seat opposite her, and in the light she could make out his features. He was a handsome man of about twenty with thick brown hair and a chiseled face with a small goatee. He wore dark sunglasses and was dressed in the Common Good officer uniform, but his left shoulder bore two orange stripes, which was the mark of the First Lieutenant status. Mrs. Xiomy had said in the cell that besides the Inspector, the First Lieutenant was the most feared man in the army.

Aurora looked into his face and there was something familiar about him but she couldn't put her finger on how she knew him. He eyed the camera and started speaking.

"Aurora Alvarez, you are hereby charged with conspiracy against the IDEAL and the Common Good government. How do you plead?"

She looked at him curiously and stated, "I will not speak without my lawyer present."

"So you plead guilty."

Aurora looked flabbergasted and repeated, "I have rights to an attorney."

The First Lieutenant thrust his fist against the table forcefully, causing the table to shake almost as much as Aurora's legs. "You gave up your rights once you conspired against your government."

Aurora's mouth was open in shock.

"I have not conspired against anything. I am guilty of breaking and entering. I admit it. I was curious and wanted to read a book. I am sorry."

The First Lieutenant stood up and whispered maliciously in her ear, "You and I both know that being curious is not the only thing you are guilty of."

Aurora's heart felt like it was beating out of her chest, and sweat was pouring down her face. It was suffocating in that room with no air circulation; she stared at the blank white walls for something or someone to help her.

He sat down across from her, void of any emotions, and resumed his normal tone of voice. "You have something that we want, Miss Alvarez. A weapon that is of catastrophic proportions. You want to help your friend Boreas and your teacher Mrs. Xiomy, don't you? If you tell us what we want to know, I will let them go free. You can go back to your home on Wishbone Avenue. Nobody needs to get hurt."

Aurora gulped and said, "How can I believe you?"

He smiled sadistically and sneered, "Am I not a trustworthy man, Miss Alvarez? Let's see how trustworthy you are. I mean to put you to the test. If you don't tell me what I want to know in the next thirty seconds, your friend Boreas is going to be given an electric shock. One may not kill him, but each thirty seconds that passes after that, I will give the order to give him another, and then another. You can see where I am going with this."

Aurora couldn't believe what she was hearing. The First Lieutenant pressed a button and the white wall in front of her became transparent so that she was able to see into the room next to her. Horrified, she saw Boreas, shirtless and bound to a wooden chair, strapped in with electrodes taped to his chest. He was blindfolded and couldn't see her. She started to scream his name, but the First Lieutenant silenced her, saying the room was soundproof.

"Now tell me, where is the giant?"

Aurora felt her body shaking, and her mind was whirling, trying to think of something to say. She thought about Otus, but she couldn't give him up, especially if he was the one to prevent the Geometric Storm. Time was ticking away, and the Inspector had his finger on the button to send the electric current into Boreas's body. She looked into the heartless face of the First Lieutenant, who was not wavering. "Twenty-eight, twenty-nine..."

He was one number away, the button about to ignite the electric current, when she cried out, "Stop!"

The First Lieutenant grabbed her by the shirt collar and cried out, "Tell me what I want to know!"

"Please don't hurt him!"

"Where is the giant?"

Aurora started sobbing and declared, "I must tell the Inspector. He needs to know the truth. I will tell him everything about the giant and the prophecy."

The First Lieutenant released his hold on her and went to the door. He informed the guards to stop the experiment and ordered them to lead Boreas and Mrs. Xiomy back to their cell. He would take Aurora to the Inspector personally.

He grabbed her roughly and whispered into her ear, "If you are lying, the Inspector's wrath will be much worse than anything I would have made you suffer."

Aurora was handcuffed and forcefully led into a clear glass elevator that would lead up to the penthouse office of Inspector Herald. As they were propelled upward, Aurora looked down upon the town of Candlewick, and she spotted her house and near it, the house of Mary Fray. It was then that she looked up at the First Lieutenant, his sunglasses now propped on the top of his head, and she saw Mary's owl eyes staring back at her. She gasped, short of breath, and looked again. He stood there staunch and steadfast, but there was no mistake that this man before her was Mary Fray's brother. A wave of hope swept over her and she quickly checked the four corners of the glass elevator but did not see a camera. She took a deep breath and knew that their life depended on her to be brave.

She whispered, "Where is Mary?"

He obstinately turned to her with shock written over his face. "Did I instruct you to speak?"

"You are Mary Fray's brother. She was my best friend and was taken away by the Common Good army. How are you working for them? What has happened to her and your parents?"

He closed his eyes and when they opened again they were cold as ice. "That name and those people are dead to me. They couldn't let their religion go like I could. They had to make trouble and practice their Jewish faith even when I warned them what would happen. They didn't listen."

"Where is Mary? Is she dead?"

He shook his head. "No, she is not dead. She is in a jail out west."

"She is your sister."

"I warn you do not look to me for help! I do what I am told. I couldn't help my own sister. What makes you think I would risk everything for her friend?"

Aurora realized they were nearly at the top and quickly said, "If you cannot help me then tell my father. He will know what to do. But just know that if Boreas and I don't get out of here there will be worse consequences. The Geometric Storm is coming, and only we can stop it. If you care about this country, can you do this for me? For Mary's sake?"

He stared at her, and for a brief moment a look of tenderness was perceptible in his eyes. But before he could answer the elevator doors swung open, and he roughly grabbed her by the arm and led her into Inspector Herald's penthouse office. There were no walls, only large windows that ran the perimeter of the office, overlooking the town of Candlewick and the ocean beyond. TV monitors were hanging from the ceiling broadcasting all of the different channels. A solitary mahogany desk stood against the center window with a door leading onto the balcony where a telescope was sitting. She remembered the rumor that the Inspector would use the telescope to look into the graveyard and gaze upon David Xiomy's tombstone. She never thought that she would ever see this firsthand.

The First Lieutenant entrusted her into the hands of two burly officers who appeared to be the Inspector's body guards.

"She is ready to confess to the Inspector. He has been notified."

Before she could steal another look toward him for help, the First Lieutenant had signed over his prisoner and marched to the elevator, where he descended away from her. She closed her eyes, knowing that he belonged to the Inspector. Any love he had for his sister was forgotten.

The officer pointed his gun at her and ordered her to walk forward. She obliged and started inching her way through the Inspector's mighty office. It was eerily quiet at this level with all of the television sets on mute, though they were flickering as the television anchors were reciting the news. A picture of Aurora flashed onto the screen. Below it read, "IDEAL Conspirator."

The officer jabbed his gun into her back as she was nearly onto the balcony and had yet to see the Inspector.

"Miss Alvarez, come join me."

It was the same cold, manipulating voice she had heard outside her house on Wishbone Avenue and countless times on the television set. She saw him standing there behind the telescope, having been lost in the shadows of the night. The Inspector's authoritative tone ushered her forward, walking through the clear sliding door, which lead onto the majestic balcony. She looked down the thirty stories but felt dizzy. The Inspector eyed her curiously, and she was intimidated in his presence. His bald scalp was glowing in the moonlight, and his scarred face caused her to recoil slightly.

"It is nice to see you again, Miss Alvarez. Glad to hear that you will be cooperating, unlike those foolish friends of yours."

"I come to you, Inspector, because I believe that you care about this country."

"More than anything, Miss Alvarez." A cool, crisp wind nipped her as he spoke, and she hugged the wall, fearful to get too close to the banister. All he had to do was push her over and she would plunge to her death.

Aurora cleared her throat. "There is going to be a Geometric Storm that is going to hit this country. This weapon that you are looking for is the only one who can stop it. We need to help him. You need to let us fulfill our mission or else a catastrophic event will occur. Many people will die."

The Inspector chortled. "The Aurora Borealis. Oh, I have heard this prophecy before, Miss Alvarez."

"So if you know it to be true, then you must believe me and know that I am not conspiring against you. I just want to help prevent this storm."

"And I have news for you," the Inspector interjected, looking through his telescope at the world below. "I welcome this storm with open arms. I have no intention of stopping it."

Aurora felt the world spinning out of control and couldn't believe her ears. "You don't want to stop it?"

The Inspector turned to face her, seductively licking the lower half of his chipped tooth. "I am not an evil man, Miss Alvarez. I lived through such evil and war that your innocent mind cannot imagine. Before your time I saw brother killing brother due to having different religious beliefs. I saw such massacres and death over religion. I created this new country out of nothing. We had to fight people like David Xiomy and his followers in order to maintain this peace.

What I do, how I maintain it, is by force. If people start to sway, if they start to question, then it will fall apart. But this Geometric Storm will seal my fate as the ruler of this country. It will bring the people back to me, especially the ones who are looking to challenge me and the IDEAL. That cannot happen, Miss Alvarez, and you and your giant friend are not going to stop me."

Aurora was terrified of this man before her. "You want to murder innocent people to stay in power?"

"It is for the greater good, Miss Alvarez," he spoke resolutely. He stepped toward her, dogmatic and domineering, and caressed her hair saying, "You are a beautiful girl Miss. Alvarez. Don't make me end your life. Tell me what I need to know. Where is your giant friend?"

She was paralyzed with fear. She opened her mouth to speak, but the signal to her brain had stopped and no words came out.

"You don't want to make an enemy of me, Miss Alvarez. Tell me what I want to know or else you can watch your friend Boreas die. Is that what you want?"

Just then they heard a commotion within the Inspector's office, and the Inspector bellowed, very displeased to have been interrupted. The First Lieutenant opened the glass door and stepped out onto the balcony.

"Excuse my intrusion, Inspector, but I just got word from Officer Woolchuck. Two prisoners have escaped."

The Inspector released his hold on Aurora and cried out, "Escaped! What do you mean escaped?"

He stormed off the balcony, enraged, slamming and locking the door behind him. He had left Aurora there, knowing there was no way of escape. Aurora regained feeling in her fingers now that the Inspector was not touching her, and she bit her nails in suspenseful anguish. Did Boreas and Mrs. Xiomy escape? Did the First Lieutenant reach out to her father like she had asked? She stood there in the whirling wind and felt herself at the mercy of the Inspector. It was hopeless. There was no chance of escape. She felt herself collapse onto the floor, and she leaned her head against the brick thinking there was no hope left. She clung tightly to the ledge, wearily thinking about her parents. She was glad she wrote the letter and told them how much she loved them. She couldn't remember the last time she had told them that, but she did love them very much. And now she may never see them again to tell them that in person. She would be found dead, along with Boreas, and no one would stop the Geometric Storm from transpiring.

Aurora looked up and appeared to be floating through time, the sky illuminated by the colorful glow of the northern lights. Flashes of light were streaming from the sun in a multitude of colors toward Candlewick with its power conquering all in its path. The ocean was the color of blood; fish and other ocean life were floating on the surface, destroyed by the radiation. And then she saw her parents lying on the shore, their bodies being buried by the waves.

She snapped out of her hallucination with a start. The Inspector still had not come back, and she thought she was hearing her name resonate in the wind. She sat huddled in her corner, her arms wrapped around her chest to keep herself warm, but then she froze as she heard another sound reverberating below the balcony walls. She listened again.

"Aurora!"

It was her name being called out loud and clear. She rose to her feet and looked cautiously over the edge of the balcony when all of a sudden she gasped as something large propelled straight toward her. It came into focus, and before she knew it she was swooped up into a giant hand and was flying upward toward the sky.

Chapter 10

Plymouth Tartarus

"**O**tus what are you doing here?" she cried out, not believing this was happening.

"Glad to see you too!" He smiled and propped her into the overalls pocket where Mrs. Xiomy was lying down, passed out. Aurora quickly hurried to her side and tried to shake her awake out of her fainting spell.

Aurora looked up at Otus and asked, "Where is Boreas?"

"He is safe. He'll explain everything once we get there."

"Once we get where?"

Mrs. Xiomy came out of her unconscious state and then screamed a high, piercing scream that turned into a fit of hysterical laughter. Mrs. Xiomy then fainted again and was lying lifeless in Otus's pocket, her head leaning against Aurora's chest. Otus continued taking huge leaps into the air, and in the distance Aurora could make out sirens signaling their escape. Fear once again overwhelmed her knowing that the Inspector would be looking for them. She clutched onto Mrs. Xiomy's hand until they reached the Candlewick Park cave where Otus had been hiding for the past three days. Aurora spotted the Fiat hidden in the forsythia bushes, and she felt her heart skip a beat knowing that Boreas must have driven it here. Did he even have a license? She hoped Newton was all right.

Otus removed the wooden panel and started to trudge through the cave, and Aurora searched madly for Boreas, but he was nowhere to be found.

"Otus, where is he?" she asked fearful that Boreas was not as fortunate as them with their narrow escape.

Otus smiled back. "Boreas is safe. You will see him in a minute. We have to get out of this cave before it fills with water."

She had no idea what he was talking about as they headed deeper into the dark cold cave. The water was up to Otus's ankles, and he had to duck in order to not hit his head on the top of the cave ceiling. There were some graffiti art on the sides of the cave that was barely legible that read, "No Trespassing" and "Haunted." There was nothing and no one else in that cave. They reached the solid wall foundation at the back, and it was a dead end. The water was now gushing with great velocity into the cave due to high tide and was already up to Otus's waistline. There was nowhere else to turn. The water continued to rise, inching higher and higher. Otus pushed on the cave wall, and it appeared to be moving. It was not the end of the cave wall at all but an illusion, and before she could comprehend this fact, the granite wall continued opening like elevator doors and revealed a glass structure that was as large as the cave wall itself. Otus took a careful step onto the glass floor of the contraption, and the cave walls started to close them in like a sarcophagus. A grated floor drained the water out of the contraption that they were now in. It was pitch dark, and Aurora began to feel as if they were trapped. Just then the walls began to vibrate, and Aurora dug her nails into Otus's skin, alarmed, as they started to plummet downward into the Atlantic Ocean.

"We are going under!" Aurora cried out in disbelief. "We will be killed!"

Otus laughed heartily. "That's what I thought too! But I'm still here. Unless it's my ghost that is carrying you."

Aurora didn't have a choice but to trust Otus as the elevator continued to submerge beneath sea level and shot out like a rocket from the cave and into the ocean.

Aurora could not believe that she could breathe. She was sure that her lungs would collapse from the pressure like so many deep sea divers she had read about. However, oxygen pumped into her lungs just as it would on land. They continued to travel on a vertical course, and the glass elevator cast a minimal amount of light as it illuminated sea turtles, fish, and beautiful coral and anemone swaying with the ocean current. The elevator itself was a remarkable invention, octagonal in shape with each panel made out of glass, and though electronically run, it did not have any wires attached. It was being controlled by a central hub.

As Aurora stared downward she caught sight of their destination coming into focus. It was like an emerald palace sitting on the bed of the ocean floor, made out of glass and shimmering. She realized that the elevator was leading them toward this mysterious place that went against all logic, and Aurora had to blink multiple times, expecting this manifestation to disappear. The elevator was sucked through a long tube that eventually stopped abruptly. A cool mist soaked them, squirting out from the vents, and Aurora realized it was a disinfectant. She kept thinking that at any minute she would pinch herself and be back in her bed in Candlewick and not 6,500 feet below sea level on the Abyssal Plain, the deepest, most level part of the ocean.

The glass doors lifted upward and Otus stepped forth into the metropolis. Large rectangular windows acted as walls and stretched upward until they met at a cupola in the center. Aurora felt like she was in a huge undersea aquarium. Behind these walls were fish and other sea life that swam past, unfazed by this edifice. She appeared to be in a grand library with spiraled staircases elegantly draped in red velvet leading to rows upon rows of bookshelves. People were busy in motion, dressed in strange garments. Some wore brown robes that stretched down to their feet. Others wore all black with white collars. Some wore black hats, and their beards were grown long and in crises-crossed shapes. Some women wore garments that completely covered their faces and other women were dressed in long, flowing black garments but with a white neckline. Some wore beautiful Indian garments like she had seen in the portrait of Mrs. Taboo. And then she saw people dressed just like her and Mrs. Xiomy, reading or speaking in small groups turning to look at the giant and the trespassers. Some looked upon them with curious glances, while others stared up at them both paranoid and suspicious. They all stopped talking as they passed, and the men and women in their hooded clothing appeared even angry as they approached.

One man in a hooded garment stepped forth and called out in a shaky voice, "Hello. I am Charlton, the Great Secretary of Plymouth Tartarus. I am here to relay a message that the High Magistrate is waiting for you in the chapel."

Otus smiled and thanked the hooded man, who made a slight bow and then scampered off to another group who were huddled together and whispering and pointing at the giant. Mrs. Xiomy had woken up at this point and was in awe at the surroundings. Her mouth gaped open as Otus marched past people, and she pointed at one and said slowly, "I know that person. I know that person too. I thought they were both dead!"

She grabbed Aurora by the shirt collar and whispered excitedly, "Are we dead?"

Aurora stared down at the suspicious people gaping at them with books in hand. She then saw one girl about her own age, with red hair and bright green eyes. What caught her eye was not her appearance but the golden cross-shaped necklace draped around her neck. The cross was the symbol of Christianity, to remember the man Jesus and how he died. She had read about it but had never witnessed anyone wearing it before. The girl smiled up at her, and Aurora smiled back.

"I think we're in heaven," she replied.

Otus came to two large bronze doors with carvings etched into each of the squares.

"The Holy Door from St. Peter's Basilica!" Mrs. Xiomy gasped, shifting in Otus's palm to get a closer look as they passed. "Yes, it is! I saw it when I was a girl in Rome. This is impossible!"

They walked into a chamber even more exuberant and opulent compared to the room Aurora had witnessed before. This room had no open windows, but each corner of the ceiling and walls were covered with art, glorious paintings that Aurora had never seen before. At the center of the ceiling was an old man with a white beard, reaching out to touch the finger of a young nude man as if life was being ignited through their fingertips.

"The Sistine Chapel," Mrs. Xiomy gasped in awe at the magnificent room they were walking into. Aurora thought she might faint again, but instead she was craning her neck as far back as it could go to take in this unbelievable image.

"Otus, where are we?" Aurora asked, seeing a small Asian woman standing on the altar, wearing a bright yellow dress and a headdress of shells that draped down over her long black hair. She had big oval eyes and an olive complexion, and she was smiling up at the visitors as they approached her altar. Otus gently placed

Aurora and Mrs. Xiomy down in front of her, and they stared at this woman, not sure whether they should speak or wait to be spoken to. The woman looked familiar, but Aurora couldn't place where she had met her before.

"Thank you Otus. So glad you all arrived safely."

Mrs. Xiomy looked at the woman, and then her eyes opened wide in recognition. "Fawn, is it really you?"

"Surprised you still remember me, my old friend."

"Remember you! Remember this!" She whirled around in circles at the Sistine Chapel. "This was destroyed. You all were destroyed." Mrs. Xiomy then turned as if bitterly afraid and continued meekly, "And it was my fault."

The woman named Fawn looked down at her with intense tenacity. "Of all the things I would love to say to you right now… but behold, we have company."

She turned to Aurora, who was standing there holding onto Otus's hand for protection.

"And who are you?"

Aurora let go of Otus and stepped forward. "My name is Aurora Alvarez. Please, I was told my friend was here. Boreas Stockington. Where is he?"

Fawn stepped back at the name but then quickly recovered. "Your friend is safe. We will take you to him shortly."

"How was the reunion?" Mrs. Xiomy mumbled.

"Went as well as you'd expect after ten years."

Aurora watched the two women who continued to stare each other down. She turned to Otus's beaming green eyes for help, but he merely shrugged.

"Where are we?" she finally asked, not being able to take this secrecy any longer.

"Why, you are in Plymouth Tartarus, or the lowest region of the Underworld."

"You came up with that all on your own?" Mrs. Xiomy heckled.

"We all came up with it." Fawn ignored Mrs. Xiomy's sarcasm. "Aurora, this place will not be found on any of your maps, and we intend to keep it that way. We are the new age puritans, come here to worship freely away from the United States of the Common Good. This is our new country."

Otus turned around and his head nearly was able to reach the top of the Sistine Chapel. "Are each of these panels stories?" he asked bewildered, looking from panel to panel.

"Biblical stories," Fawn responded. "They were created by a painter named Michelangelo in the Renaissance Era. When they destroyed the Vatican we had to risk our lives to save this. We took it down panel by panel and put it in our submarine, sonar protected, of course."

"How did you get access?" Mrs. Xiomy asked. "I thought the guards were blocking anyone from entering or leaving."

"Well, the pope and the priests covered for us. They joined our cause and allowed us to use the secret passage from the Vatican to the Castel Sant'Angelo. The Swiss guards swore an oath to protect the pope. We lost many a brave man during that night."

"To preserve a story?" Aurora looked up both perplexed and mesmerized. "They are beautiful stories."

"They are something we would want our children and grandchildren to see one day, right, Fawn?" Mrs. Xiomy chided.

Fawn didn't answer and instead walked gracefully to a locked cabinet labeled "Church Tabernacle" and took out a long necklace made out of sea shells.

"Here, Otus." He knelt down and bent his head so large in proportion to Fawn's small frame. "I welcome you as our visitor to Plymouth Tartarus."

She placed the sea shells around his neck, and the sea shells jangled as he rose to his full height. He admired each of the shells in his hands.

"They represent all faiths as one." She smiled, and Aurora watched this commemoration with great apprehension. Did they know of Otus's place in this puzzle, of his mission that Aurora and Boreas were on?

Fawn next led them through a long corridor, and everyone they passed stopped and looked up at the giant. Fawn and Mrs. Xiomy continued to give each other the cold shoulder; there was such friction between these two women. Aurora knew that she had to stay observant because this strange land was so foreign, yet illegal in so many ways. To speak the name of God so openly was a reason to be locked up for life, if not murdered for spreading the lies. She recalled the story of the author, Thomas Young, who had posted the story of Jesus over the Internet and how quickly he was made to suffer the consequences. What would happen to everyone down here if they were ever discovered? Aurora knew the answer, and she knew that they were all aware of it too.

They entered a large hall where the Bible, the Koran, and the Torah were all lined up side by side. All the original texts, Fawn explained as they walked past. People were on their knees praying to these books, and Aurora couldn't help but watch the old and the young chanting and saying their prayers out loud in unison. What a strange world where people prayed to relics and books. But then she thought, didn't they do the same thing but for the IDEAL? And they didn't even know who the IDEAL was, just that to go against the IDEAL was wrong.

Beside the Torah was the symbol that Mary had made on Joshua's Laundromat; the two triangles interwoven as one to make a star shape, or hexagram. Aurora turned to Fawn and asked, "What is that drawing? What does it mean?"

Fawn smiled and said, "That is the Star of David. Also known in Hebrew as the Shield of David. It is a symbol of Judaism."

They continued past the prayer books and came across a platinum white door that bore the name "Sanctuary" in metallic print. But it was anything but a peaceful sanctuary because they heard a voice screaming at the top of its lungs within. Fawn opened the door and there, to Aurora's relief, was Boreas yelling at two hooded men trying to serve him food.

"I swear I won't eat until I find out that my friends are all right!"

As the door swung open, Aurora laughed as she watched Boreas knock a plate of food to the ground, and the hooded figures quickly picked up the scraps. Boreas's eyes met Aurora's, and he smiled wide, reassured that she was alive. His eyes then wandered to Aurora's left, where Fawn stepped forward from behind her, and a scowl transformed over his features. Fawn's placid voice rang out in the small chamber, "Your friends are here safely."

She left before anyone could say another word. Boreas continued to stare menacingly as she left, and Aurora went to his side in a hurry. Because it was that moment she realized why Fawn looked so familiar. She was the spitting image of Boreas.

Chapter 11

Secrets Revealed

*A*urora nearly tackled Boreas and both of them fell over in laughter. She threw her arms around him, so happy that he was all right.

"I thought that Otus wouldn't have found you in time," he said wearily.

"I am fine." Aurora smiled. "And Mrs. Xiomy now believes in giants."

"As well as a few other things," Mrs. Xiomy replied hastily. "I am glad you are all right."

Aurora turned to Boreas flabbergasted and exclaimed, "But how did you escape? How did you find the cave and warn Otus?"

Boreas took a deep breath and then relayed the story from the beginning.

The guards had led both Boreas and Mrs. Xiomy back to the prison cell when they were intercepted by the First Lieutenant. He demanded custody once again of the prisoners, and they overheard him tell the Common Good officers that he wasn't convinced that Aurora would do as she promised and provide the whereabouts of the giant. He growled at the prisoners to accompany him into an adjacent room to await word from the Inspector's penthouse office. They walked in, but the First Lieutenant closed the door abruptly behind him. Sitting at the desk, disguised as a Common Good officer, was Mr. Alvarez, Aurora's father. The First Lieutenant quickly whispered something into Mr. Alvarez's ear and then exited the room without any explanation. Boreas had tried to interject, but Mr. Alvarez said that there wasn't any time to explain.

Mr. Alvarez instructed Mrs. Xiomy to wait in the interrogation room, to stall for time, and then he methodically hit two panels in the white wall, which was not a wall at all but a secret door that lead into a hidden chamber. Boreas was ordered to follow Mr. Alvarez into the hollow chamber that turned into a dank and dark tunnel. They cautiously meandered their way down the long, narrow tunnel and Boreas could hear cars overhead but couldn't decipher which road they were under. His shoes started to splash into puddles, which was when he noticed that the tunnel was leading them to the Candlewick Brook that emptied out next to the graveyard. There, before his eyes, was Mrs. Xiomy's Fiat, waiting for him; All their stuff still in the trunk. Mr. Alvarez ordered Boreas to drive and find the giant. He said that once he found the giant, they were to come back and rescue Mrs. Xiomy, who would be waiting for them in the graveyard near David Xiomy's gravesite.

Boreas sped off to the Candlewick Park cave, but when he got there Otus had disappeared. Frantically he ran to the back of the cave, following Otus's footprints until he discovered that they ended at a dead end of solid rock. He traced his hand over the drawings and discovered the trigger that initiated the hidden glass elevator. He travelled through the ocean in the glass contraption until he found himself in Plymouth Tartarus.

"That is when I found Otus and told him to hurry and rescue you both."

Mrs. Xiomy cleared her throat, wanting to continue the story at this point. Boreas relented, grateful to catch his breath.

She licked her lips and continued the tale. "While Boreas went to get to Otus, I was stuck stalling for time. Officer Woolchuck got suspicious and came into the interrogation room, catching Mr. Alvarez coming back through the hidden chamber. He was about to warn the other guards when I hit him square across the jaw and he went down."

She showed off her right knuckles, which were slightly bruised from the hit. Boreas rolled his eyes at his teacher bragging about her violent tendencies.

"I then fled with Mr. Alvarez down the secret corridor; by this time the alarm had sounded. Mr. Alvarez told me to run to the gate, and he stayed behind to barricade the door and prevent anyone from coming through. I ran through the sewer, which emptied out into the brook near the graveyard. Then it looked as if all the lights had gone out, so I looked up, fearful it was the Inspector's planes coming to swoop in and grab me, but it wasn't a plane but a large hand reaching out for me. I screamed and..."

"Passed out," Aurora chimed in.

"I prefer 'gracefully fell,'" Mrs. Xiomy said unabashedly.

"And then after I found Mrs. Xiomy, I found you." Otus smiled triumphantly. "Exactly where Boreas told me you would be."

Aurora was wide-eyed in amazement. "I can't believe my father did all that. He risked everything to help us escape!"

Mrs. Xiomy nodded. "And he probably would be very upset if we all died of hunger."

Otus took that as a cue to eat and plopped down, the floor shaking beneath his weight. Aurora and Boreas, both not having eaten in three days, started picking at the buffet spread before them. They heartily chewed down the mussels, prawns, salmon, bread, and water.

Boreas reached into his pocket and retrieved a handkerchief that Aurora immediately recognized as her father's. His initials were embroidered on the far right corner. Boreas said in mid-bite, "Your father wanted you to have this."

Aurora grabbed it out of his hand. It read:

> *My dear Aurora,*
>
> *If you are reading this, then I know you are safe. No one could have predicted that you and Boreas are the answers to the prophecy, but if it is so, I could not be prouder of you. I know that you will be able to help fulfill this mission and bring peace to this country and to the people once again. Do not worry about me or your mother. We will find a way through this. You need to take care of yourself, and I hope that we will see your beautiful face again when this is over. Know that we love you very much, and remember to look to the stars and trust in your heart. Te quiero mi hermosa hija.*

Aurora wiped a tear from her eye and put the handkerchief safely into her pocket. She then relayed her encounter with the Inspector. Both Otus and Boreas looked at each other dumbfounded, especially after Aurora described in detail the Inspector's desire for the Geometric Storm to hit. Mrs. Xiomy was not surprised. She shook her head at the amateurs before her.

"Like I told you both, you cannot trust anyone, especially not the Inspector."

Boreas's eyes darted toward the closed door where Fawn, the High Magistrate, had exited. "You're right. Not anyone."

Aurora took this as her cue to ask the question she was dreading. "Boreas, is the High Magistrate your mother?"

"Your mom?" Otus nearly choked on the water he was gulping down. "But I thought she was killed ten years ago?"

"So did I!" Boreas slammed his fork down onto the glass plate and stood up, facing the opposite end of the room.

The room went silent, and no one dared to take a bite or even swallow. Boreas continued staring out through the glass porthole and took a deep breath, "When I came out of the glass elevator, the Great Secretary wouldn't let Otus leave and come rescue you, Aurora, until I met with the High Magistrate. They didn't trust any outsiders and needed to be sure that it wasn't a trap. So I ran into the Sistine Chapel, pushing people out of the way and screaming that this High Magistrate had to let Otus go, that he had to rescue my friends. And there she was, standing there with that stupid shell headdress. She stared at me as if I was a ghost. I thought she was for an instant. My mother, who I thought was dead, has been here all this time!" He kicked the table with all his strength, and a plate of food crashed to the floor. "She still is dead to me!"

He charged toward the door and slammed it shut behind him. Aurora got up to run after him, but Otus put his foot up, blocking the exit.

"Leave him be, Aurora," he said.

Mrs. Xiomy took a giant bite out of her bread and then gargled some water in her throat. "She's an idiot for leaving him to begin with. Continuing on with her rebellion. There is no rebellion anymore. The cause is dead. Died with my husband."

Aurora resumed her place at the table. "Why does the High Magistrate hate you so much?"

Mrs. Xiomy turned bright red. "Is it that obvious? Well, I guess it must be. I mean, if fifteen years can't heal past wounds than nothing will, huh?" She took a deep breath. "We used to be best friends.

I mean, growing up on the same block and everything. She was Buddhist; I was Muslim. But that never mattered to us, even when there was all the fighting and the religious war broke out over the world. We were there for each other. We joined the revolution together. And then we fell in love with the same man—David Xiomy, who ended up falling in love with me. Fawn didn't take the news lightly. We got into a huge fight, and she left the rebellion. Later I found out that she had married Henry Stockington from Wishbone Avenue. They had two sons, one being your friend Boreas. Five years after his birth there was that terrible fire at the Candlewick prison where she was assisting the Professor with experimental work for the government. They never found her body, but it was assumed that she had died, along with some of my other friends from the rebellion. But somehow I always knew she didn't die. She was too much of a fighter, that one. That's why she always insisted that David made the wrong decision. She said that if it was her, she never would have given up the rebellion for a man. Maybe I am weak. I don't know. But when you're in love, you do some things that go against your nature. Against nature itself."

Otus handed Mrs. Xiomy a handkerchief, and she blew her nose in it. Aurora watched her, mystified, and then looked to Otus, who was reading a book on one of the bookshelves. He read it so fast that the pages were whirling past, creating a breeze. He then picked up another book and did the same thing.

"Are you able to read that fast?" she asked picking up each of the books that he was dropping on the floor: Koran, the Old Testament, the New Testament, and the Vedas.

"Yeah. Can't you read this fast?"

She shook her head as she opened one of the book covers. "It would take me at least a week to read one of these books, if not longer. We read it page by page."

"That's what I do too," he said, giving a demonstration with a book he had just picked up. He then flipped through the pages like a flip book and then slammed it shut. "See? Page by page."

Aurora then picked up the Koran and started to read it. Otus tapped his foot as she proceeded with reading the first page silently in her head.

"Are you done yet?"

"Halfway."

"With just one page? No wonder you humans are such trouble. If you were able to read faster like me you could use that knowledge for more good than evil."

"The Common Good says books cause more evil than good. They give people ideas. They want us to share one idea."

"Mrs. Taboo says that we all have different ideas. It's the people who act on their ideas that show whether they are evil or good. We can all go in either direction."

Aurora nodded, looking at Mrs. Xiomy, who had gotten into a conversation with one of the cloaked men that she recognized.

Aurora looked up at her friend and asked, "Otus, did you ever hear of a book that describes the Geometric Storm and the prophecy? It was something that Mrs. Xiomy's husband mentioned before his death, and he predicted that we would find each other. I have a feeling that either you or Mrs. Taboo knows about this."

He leaned back against the wall and nearly hit his head on one of the bookshelves. His left eyebrow shot up toward the tip of his head as he tried to extrapolate this piece of knowledge from his brain.

"There is a book," he finally said. His eyelids fluttered as if in a trance. "The last time I saw Mrs. Taboo, she came down to the house and brought the conch shell with her. She said that this shell would lead me to you. I asked her how she knew. She said that she had read about it, and it was a reliable source. I had asked her how she knew, and she replied that he is the last remaining heir of the Gassendis. His ancestor predicted this while gazing at the northern lights."

"Pierre Gassendi?" Aurora gasped. "He is the one who named the northern lights as *Aurora Borealis*. His long lost relative is the man we need to find. He must be the one who has the book. Do you know where Mrs. Taboo is? Is she down here?"

Otus shook his head. "No, she's not here. Her conch shell was the last gift she gave me. She said she was travelling north to wait there until you and Boreas have inherited your gifts."

She tugged on Otus's sleeve, and he picked her up so that she was right near his ear cavity. Mrs. Xiomy was still deep in conversation with the cloaked man, so Aurora quickly said, "I don't know if we can trust these people. I don't think they know about our mission, but I could be mistaken. They might have an agenda of their own for you, but we need to still get you to the northern lights. But first we need to find out who this long-lost heir is. We'll bide our time, but please don't say anything to anyone about our mission. Okay?"

He winked back at her. "You got it. Now on with my reading."

She was carried back to the ground when the door shot open. She expected Boreas, but it was a man who entered. He was the man Charlton who had announced that they needed to go to the chapel when Aurora had first entered this strange place. Now that she was face to face with him, he appeared much more inept and spineless.

He bowed and then proclaimed, "In case you have forgotten, I am the Great Secretary of Plymouth Tartarus and proclaim that you are all invited to our gala tomorrow night in the Great Hall. We will have outfits prepared for you to wear. Weren't there four of you?"

"He'll be back in a minute," Aurora quickly chimed in.

The Great Secretary nodded. "We are having our people create an outfit especially for you, giant. Two of our head seamstresses will be here to measure you all and make sure that they have the proportions correct."

Otus bowed down to the Great Secretary, but Charlton took a step back, horrified, and immediately scrambled out of the room.

Otus shrugged. "I always have that effect on people."

Aurora and Mrs. Xiomy laughed. The two cloaked figures left and two young girls entered. One had auburn hair with bangs that swept over her eyes. She was wearing a golden frock with lace along the edges. The other was the fiery redheaded girl with the cross that Aurora remembered when they were carried into the hall. She was wearing a beautiful emerald frock with golden trim. She smiled heartily at her when they walked in. The auburn-haired girl spoke with an Irish accent, a scowl over her beautiful features.

"My name is Babs O'Hara, and this is my sister Eileen. We are here to get your measurements for the gala tomorrow night."

Eileen stepped forward and offered her hand to both Mrs. Xiomy and Aurora. She then looked up and offered her hand to Otus, who recalled the lesson from Aurora and said, "Are we shaking on it?"

Eileen giggled. "Shaking hands is also to say 'How do you do?'"

Otus nodded, taking this in, and then offered his hand to Eileen. Babs was busy getting out her measuring tape and started with taking down the proportions of Mrs. Xiomy, who was complaining that she couldn't remember the last time she wore a ball gown.

"I think the last fancy dress I wore was on my wedding day. And that wasn't fancy at all. I bought it for $25 since it was wartime. We got married by a priest in the ancient woods. Probably was one of the last religious ceremonies of our time."

Eileen shook her head. "We have religious ceremonies down here. Babs will be married later this month to Josh Schroeder."

"She means there aren't any religious ceremonies on the mainland." Babs huffed as she took Aurora's measurements hastily.

Aurora watched her curiously and asked, "You are both around my age. When did you come down here? How did you find out about it?"

Babs ignored her and made a few markings on her clipboard. She then proceeded toward Otus, not even flinching and took out an extra-long measuring tape. She handed the two edges to Otus and instructed him to wrap the tape around his waist. Otus attempted to but only got a quarter of the way around his large torso. Babs nodded and then made a note in her clipboard. "Multiplying by four, that makes 320 inches. Now put it at the top of your shoulder blade and let it hang down.

She climbed onto a ladder near the bookshelf and made a mark at a point on his belly where the measuring tape landed. Otus was getting a kick out of this whole process.

While this was going on, Eileen turned to Aurora and said, "I was born here. Babs came here when she was two years old with my parents. They were escaping from the religious persecution after the rebellion fell. They weren't willing to give up their Catholic beliefs. It's the same story for so many here. Most ended up in jail and arrested. Others gave up their beliefs once their loved ones were seized and tortured. Then there were my parents, who weren't able to just give up. There was a rumor about a new world that was being built under the ocean, the only unexplored and unchartered territory of the United States of the Common Good. My mother was pregnant with me and my father didn't want to take the chance, but my mother said she would prefer they die trying than have us be raised in a world without God or freedom.

"So they ended up sneaking out at the Sacred Hour to the Cliffs of Moore. Others were there waiting for the cue. A bright neon blue light shone out from the water, and everyone watched as this giant torpedo-like submarine emerged. Just then gunshots rang out, and people started screaming. Everyone dove into the water and swam for their lives as bullets shot their townspeople and friends down one by one. My parents, with God's help, managed to make it out to the center of the ocean. They swam toward the submarine and were hoisted inside and carried back here with about 100 others. The submarine did the same thing for every country that it could get to, for those brave enough to start a new life as Puritans, for everyone to be welcomed no matter what your belief."

"Prisoners is more like it," Babs spit out, the measuring tape in her mouth as she was trying to estimate Otus's shoe size. "We aren't allowed to leave this place."

"Babs, stop it. Please don't mind her."

Babs turned to Aurora and laughed. "You think you are leaving here. Guess again, my friend. They won't risk you telling on their precious hideaway."

Just then the door swung open, and Boreas entered. He froze when he saw Babs and Eileen staring at him. Embarrassed, he turned to leave but Aurora called him back.

"Boreas, this is Eileen and Babs. They are taking our measurements for the gala tomorrow night."

Boreas laughed. "I'm not going to their little gala. I am leaving this place, and so are you, Aurora. Otus, come on."

Otus instead took another book off of the bookshelf. "Sorry, Boreas, but we're not leaving until after the gala."

Boreas went straight up to him, "Have they brainwashed you? We are leaving. I am not going to stay here another minute as my m—as they keep us down here with all their religious dogma and fake promises."

"I told you that you can't leave," Babs repeated. She took the measuring tape and put it up against Boreas's chest as he watched her with his intense gaze. "They want to keep their flock on a tight leash. And you're now part of that."

Eileen clutched onto her cross and looked upward as if asking for help. Boreas grabbed the tape measure from out of Babs's hand, and they struggled with it until Boreas won with his force and flung it across the room. Otus caught it before it hit the ground and handed it back to Babs, who accepted it gratefully.

She angrily yelled at Boreas, "No one has ever done that before!"

"Well, then it's about time that you had more people from the mainland knock some sense into you all. I am not a prisoner here, and we are going to leave here whenever we damn well want to."

Babs took hold of Eileen's arm and led her to the door. "For your sake I hope you're right. To be stuck down here with people like you for eternity would be hell."

The door slammed shut behind the two girls, and Otus laughed, "Wow, Boreas, I think she likes you."

"Shut up, Otus!" He sat down sullenly.

Mrs. Xiomy had watched the little expose with great anxiety. "I just remembered Newton is waiting for me. I hope he has enough sense to go back to the house, especially if we are to stay here for a while."

"Don't blame me," Boreas exclaimed. "I want to leave. Blame the giant who wants to party it up all night long with these religious fanatics."

Otus banged his fist against the wall, and all stepped back as part of the sheet rock crumbled around them. He grabbed Boreas, who struggled violently to get out of his clutch. "Look, Boreas, we are not leaving yet, so get it into your head. If anything I know that we were meant to find this place. And you were meant to find your mom. For whatever reason we are all meant to be right here. So put on new clothes because you are going to that gala if I need to carry you there myself."

He dropped Boreas, whose body smacked against the carpet. He rolled over onto his back and looked up into the odious eyes of Otus. His mouth hung open in disbelief, having never seen this side of Otus before.

"Fine, I'll go. Not because you are scaring me into it—because you're not—but because I need to look out for the rest of you and make sure you don't get into more trouble."

He sulkily walked to the other end of the room and stared out of the window at the ocean life swimming past. Aurora gave Otus a thumbs-up sign, and Otus gave one back, picking up on the meaning behind the gesture.

Inspector Herald took the call. It was from Officers Woolchuck and Pelican.

"You better have found them," his voice rattled into the phone.

Officer Woolchuck's voice sounded through static. "Not yet. But we did find something else. In the Candlewick Park an abandoned vehicle was found hidden in the forsythia bushes near the haunted cave."

"The cave is not haunted," the voice of Officer Pelican exclaimed, grabbing the phone out of her partner's hand. "I am sorry, Inspector. The car was near the Candlewick Park cave, and a dog was in the passenger seat with the window down. Whoever had abandoned the car did not intend to leave it for long."

"Who does the car belong to?" Inspector Herald growled.

"A Mrs. Rana Xiomy. Widow of David Xiomy."

"Of course I know whose wife she was you fool!" The Inspector started wheezing through the phone like an asthmatic having an attack. "What else did you find?"

"The footprints lead to the cave, but then they disappear. Washed away from the high tide."

"That's probably what they want us to think."

The Inspector looked into the mirror at his burned reflection. Patches of red and white scarring covered his face and his bald scalp. Where eyebrows should have been, they were stripped off, just leaving suntanned outlines, and his nose square and disfigured from plastic surgery, as if it wasn't his own. Only his lips were still intact.

"They are all still alive, and you will find them! I will relay this to the IDEAL, but use whatever methods necessary. Wherever they are, we will find that giant!"

He hung up the phone with a slam and looked out his window where there was an unmarked grave in the Candlewick Prison cemetery. Though it was lined with many rebels from the Last Straw rebellion, this one still stood out, for it was the only one with a forever plant blooming beside the tombstone. He cringed at the sight of it, screaming into the intercom and summoning his secretary into the office. She was wearing a black suit jacket and a short black skirt that caused his eyes to be distracted, staring instinctively toward her long, bare legs as they advanced toward him. She still could not look him straight in the eye even after working together for two years. He didn't question it, though, since no one except the IDEAL could ever look at his disfigured face without being terrified. Now the Inspector couldn't differentiate if they were more terrified of his appearance or his reputation.

"Miss Thompson, I thought I asked that you and your team destroy any flowers or plants buried in homage to those rebels in the cemetery."

"They have been dug out and burned upon your request," she sincerely stated, highlighting her English accent.

He pointed his finger menacingly out the window. "Then what do you call that?"

She followed his gaze, and her eyes opened wide in disbelief as the forever plant bloomed mockingly next to the unmarked grave.

"I am so sorry. I personally saw to it that it was destroyed. Someone must have planted another one. I will make sure it doesn't happen again."

He tapped his fingernails onto the desktop, like drums at a funeral procession. His voice spoke with an eerie calmness. "It better not, Miss Thompson, or else there may be a need to dig another grave in that cemetery. And we wouldn't want that, would we?"

Her lips quivered as she quickly nodded and hastened out the door, closing it abruptly behind her. The Inspector looked out the window again. Though an innocent plant, it was a reminder that even after all these years, David Xiomy was not forgotten. The rebel's prophecy was being lived out, and the Inspector had to stop it. It was for the Common Good that the Geometric Storm occur without any interference. As the IDEAL said, "It will remind them who is really in power."

David Xiomy could not prevent the Geometric Storm from taking place. The Inspector should know. He was the one who killed him fifteen years earlier. Now all that was left was a giant and two teenagers to follow their leader's fate.

Chapter 12

The Gala

Aurora twirled around in the most beautiful dress that she had ever seen. It was a deep shade of maroon, and the fabric elegantly draped down her body. Seashells were sewn into the hem of the dress. Eileen had curled her golden brown hair, pinning part of it up with a clip made out of gold. Aurora wouldn't have recognized herself if she passed her reflection in the mirror. Even her own parents wouldn't have recognized her. She doubted the town would call her Fatty Alvarez wearing this. Even Hattie Pearlton would be speechless if she saw her like this. And perhaps Jonathan Stockington would see her as something more.

She froze as she thought of Jonathan. He still was up there in Candlewick, unaware that his mother was alive. She wondered how he would take the news. Probably similar to Boreas. But then again, the two brothers were nothing alike. She thought that Jonathan would forgive his mother, while Boreas seemed not to have a forgiveness bone in his body.

Mrs. Xiomy walked in. She was wearing a stunning fitted purple dress with a sweetheart neckline, revealing a hint of cleavage. Aurora compared herself to the other woman immediately and noticed the lumps in her own stomach that were hidden beneath the cut of the dress but still noticeably there. And her large hips were more emphasized in the dress than when she wore jeans and a t-shirt.

"Eileen, do you think that maybe I should wear something else?"

"You look stunning." Eileen smiled and put her arm around Aurora's shoulders. "No eligible man in Plymouth Tartarus will be able to keep his eyes off you."

"Yeah, because I'm the fattest girl in this country," she thought, putting on the black shoes that were too small for her feet. She knew that she would have huge welts on her feet after a night of dancing. That is, if she were even asked to dance. Memories of the high school spring formal came back to haunt her as she recalled going to the dance alone and wondering if she would dance with Jonathan. She had worn a floral print dress that her mother had picked out for her. The pattern made her look like a giant cabbage patch and was not becoming to her figure, but her mother insisted that since florals looked good on her, they would work for her daughter as well.

As soon as she arrived, several of the students pointed out the large garden that had just popped up into the school gym. She was horrified and wished that she had someone she could sit with or talk to, but everyone was in their cliques, and Mary wouldn't have been caught dead at a spring formal. The girls in her class didn't even bother to speak to her, except to comment negatively on her dress. The other girls looked perfectly polished, so elegantly dressed, with their hair all styled and makeup professionally painted on their faces. She watched them dance with the boys in the center of the decorated gym as she sat in a corner. The band played slow songs and fast songs, and she was envious of all of them. Of course, Hattie looked beautiful in a blue silk dress that was just above her knee, revealing her long, thin legs. Jonathan was as handsome as ever in a white dress shirt, navy blue vest and tie, and his hair was free flowing, not in a ponytail like it normally was. She got up to get some punch and, as if it was synchronized, Jonathan also walked over to the table; their hands simultaneously touched the ladle for the punch, and she quickly removed her hand in a hurry. Jonathan smiled and poured a cup, handing it to Aurora.

"You were here first," he said, his pearly white teeth sparkling in the light. A slow song was playing and Aurora hoped he would ask her to dance. But Hattie was over before he had a chance to do anything but smile. She grabbed the cup out of Aurora's hand, saying, "Oh, I think that's for me."

She took a drink and then grabbed Jonathan's hand. "Come on, Jonathan. This is our song."

"I poured that for Aurora," he said, pulling his hand away from her.

"I thought you were just watering the flowers. You probably didn't realize there was a girl underneath that rosebush."

She then threw the rest of the punch into Aurora's face. A crowd of people started to congregate around them.

Aurora stood there, panicking, when all of a sudden a voice boomed over the loud speakers. It was Boreas, drunk and singing the song "Sweet Caroline." Everyone started laughing as he ran up and down the stage away from the band leaders, who were trying to steal the microphone out of his hands. Hattie started laughing, and Jonathan raced up on stage and tackled his brother, knocking the microphone out of his hands. Jonathan punched him, but Aurora hadn't waited to find out what else happened. The distraction was enough for her to race out of the gym before anyone else could say anything negative about her. She could only handle so much humiliation for one night. She ran all the way home, remembering how Jonathan had handed her the cup first. He had intended for it to be for her. Not for Hattie.

Aurora smoothed the beautiful maroon dress, thinking how different it would have been if she had worn this dress and not the floral one to the spring formal. Jonathan might have even asked her to dance. Things would have been really different, but that world seemed so far away at the moment. She didn't know if she would ever return to Candlewick High. She didn't know where she would be tomorrow. She just knew that she had to get through this night and find out how they could find Pierre Gassendi's heir, wherever he was.

A knock came from the door, and she heard Boreas say from the other side, "Hey, you ladies decent in there?"

Aurora smoothed out her dress one more time and sucked in her stomach. Mrs. Xiomy put a hand on her shoulder and smiled. "You look radiant, Aurora."

Boreas walked in looking so debonair that she couldn't believe her eyes. His hair was gelled to the side, and he was wearing a tuxedo that brought out his hazel eyes. He was now clean shaven, and she could see the outline of his mouth that curved upward into a beautiful smile as he looked at her.

"Hi, Aurora. You look…"

"You don't have to say anything," Aurora said, turning back toward the mirror, and nervously fidgeting with her dress.

"I meant to say you look good."

Aurora watched his reflection through the mirror. "Thanks. You do too."

His eyes danced, as he leaned to one side against the doorway. "Umm, that guy Charlton said I had to escort someone into the gala…so since we're all dressed up and everything…umm…can I escort you? Or do I need to fight a hundred other guys for the honor?"

She laughed at the playfulness of his eyes. "You just have to fight about fifty, but that should be a piece of cake for you."

She followed him out of the room and there stood Otus looking so shy and sublime. He was also dressed in a tuxedo, and Babs had gotten the proportions exactly right, despite the anguish of having to measure him. He had his hair cut slightly so that his bangs were now out of his eyes, and he wore black dress shoes.

"Otus, you look so handsome," Aurora beamed.

"I hoped you would say that." He smiled back at her, blushing. He then held out his hand toward Mrs. Xiomy. "You look ravishing, and I," he paused, trying to remember the words, "would love to have the honor of escorting you to the gala."

"Well, this is definitely a first," Mrs. Xiomy gushed. "To be escorted by a giant is definitely a new one for me. But I would be delighted."

They headed down the hall following the Great Secretary, who was looking as frazzled as ever, still dressed in his long brown robe. He had a microphone in his ear and walked at an irregular pace, suggesting that they were running behind schedule. Aurora cursed her shoes that were already scraping against the sides of her feet. She noticed a slight hole in the back of Boreas's jacket and laughed, thinking Babs got her revenge on him for stealing her measuring tape.

"Are you ready?" he asked, clutching onto her arm with more ferocity.

"Well, it will hopefully be better than the spring formal," she said softly, feeling her face already starting to perspire as they approached the bronze double doors that she'd heard Mrs. Xiomy say were from St. Patrick's Cathedral in New York City.

Boreas looked at her and smiled, "Yeah, hopefully I won't have to get in a fight for you tonight."

Startled, she inquired, "What do you mean you got in a fight for me?"

Boreas stuttered, 'What? Nothing. Forget it."

Aurora's mind rewound to the spring formal.

"Do you mean the microphone incident? The fight you had with Jonathan?"

He shook his head at her, wanting her to drop it but she wouldn't stop. "You got in that fight for me? But why? Why would you do that for me?"

"I don't know!" He faced her, taking both of her hands in his and held them tight. "Maybe because I know what it's like to have everyone against you."

The double doors opened wide and both Aurora and Boreas jumped back as a huge rush of applause erupted from the Great Hall. Fireworks were set off as they entered, and the room was flooded with an assortment of people standing in their best attire and waving to the visitors. Aurora waved back with her free hand awkwardly and followed the Great Secretary to the center of the ballroom.

Fawn was sitting on a high podium like a queen. She was wearing a long golden robe that resembled a college doctorate's hood, and the seashell headdress was still placed like a crown over her black hair, except now her long tresses were pulled up in an elegant updo. She smiled down at the visitors and raised her hand, and there immediately was silence.

"We have been blessed with four visitors into our home this evening: Otus the Giant, Mrs. Rana Xiomy, Aurora Alvarez, and Boreas Stockington."

The crowd cheered again, and Aurora felt Boreas tense up as his mother pronounced his name.

"We have not had visitors into our country, Plymouth Tartarus, in many years, and they are here as peace givers and to tell us of the outside world and of the evil we still need to face in the days and years ahead. The Common Good has grown, and the escapades of the rebellion are nearly forgotten by the youth. Only they can continue this fight for us, and we pray to whichever god or gods that we believe in for hope and for strength."

She raised her goblet to the four in the epicenter of the room.

"This song is in honor of all of you."

The band started singing, and Boreas turned to Aurora timidly and held out his hand to her.

"I think they want us to dance."

She nodded, fearful, as he put his hand on her waist, and with the other he clutched her shaking hand, intertwining his fingers with hers. He turned to look up at Otus who looked even more petrified. Boreas mouthed for him to take Mrs. Xiomy's hands, which he did, and Mrs. Xiomy shrieked slightly as he held onto her hands a little too tight.

"Just sway back and forth," Mrs. Xiomy instructed, and he nodded, thankful that she was taking the lead.

Boreas smiled at Aurora as the music started to play, and she followed him as they twirled around the beautiful marble dance floor. The chandelier illuminated a spotlight on the four of them. She felt light and free as he twirled her around the floor, not believing that she was dancing—and with a boy—in front of all these people as a guest of honor. She felt her dress floating magically with her body, in sync with the man whose body was close against her own. She felt his heart beating in rhythm with hers as they danced across the floor. She wanted to steal a glance over at Otus and Mrs. Xiomy, but her eyes were entranced, gazing deeply into Boreas's, afraid that if she lost eye contact with him, the dance would fall apart and the music would end.

The last note of the melodic song finally played, and Boreas dipped her in his arms so that his face was inches away from hers. Breathless, she leaned back, staring at his lips that were so close to her own. She felt paralyzed in his grasp, but he then lifted her back up to her feet. More applause resounded around them, and she remembered that they were not the only ones in the room. She turned and bowed to the onlookers and then to Mrs. Xiomy, who was still in one piece, with Otus having not stepped on her feet or crushed her beneath his weight. She appeared extremely relieved that the song was over and they all were ushered to their table where the feast began. Aurora quickly found a seat beside Mrs. Xiomy and Otus, not wanting to be so close to Boreas until her heart had resumed its natural beating.

Trumpets sounded as children of all ages stepped forth, carrying trays of food that they began serving to the tables. The scent of fresh fish flooded the air and everyone was talking gaily as the food was served. Everyone was enamored with Otus; every person in the room wanted a chance to speak to him or say hello. They surrounded the table and though some were a little timid at first, began to gain courage as Otus smiled down at each of the people.

"You give me and my family hope," one elderly woman said, grasping at Otus's hand. "May God bless you and your friends."

A man came up to them and shook Aurora's hand madly. He was dashing, and it appeared a smile was plastered to his face. He sat down beside Aurora and asked about the world above.

"It's been too long since I've seen it. Please tell me what it's like. I am from New Jersey. Have you been there?"

She shook her head. "I've lived in Candlewick all my life. This is the farthest I've ever travelled from there."

He nodded. "Candlewick. Is that what was Long Island?"

"Yes. Plymouth Tartarus is directly below the Candlewick Park."

"A park." The word registered, and his face lit up in remembrance. "I used to go to parks when I was a kid. Playgrounds and such. Loads of fun. And what do you believe in?"

She turned to Mrs. Xiomy, not sure how to respond. "Believe? What do you mean?"

He laughed. "Sorry, been down here too long. You don't believe in anything, do you?"

Boreas stood up and asked the man to leave.

"I didn't mean any harm. I forgot who I was talking to. It's not good to not believe in anything."

Aurora told Boreas to sit down. "I don't need your help."

He shrugged and poured another glass of wine. "Fine. I'll let all crazy religious fanatics try to convert you."

She was instantly distracted by the sight of Babs and Eileen walking arm in arm to their table. Babs was dressed in a short ivory dress, and her auburn hair was in a long braid that cascaded down her back. Eileen's red hair stuck out like a sore thumb, and it was in gentle waves over her bare shoulders, but her cross still dangled over the black mermaid styled gown. Eileen ran to Aurora's side and gushed, "You danced so beautifully. I wish I could do that. I have two left feet. That's what Babs always says."

"You did dance very well, though sorry about your choice of partner." Babs glared at Boreas, who was still sipping on his glass of wine.

"Thank you." Aurora smiled, offering them a seat across from them. "Babs, is your fiancé here?"

"Yeah, he's floating around here somewhere."

Eileen pointed out a young man in his early twenties who was with a group of boys near the band. They appeared to be rehearsing.

"Is he in the band?"

"He's a singer. He'll sing a few tunes near the end of the night. Quite boring, actually. The same two songs at every party. It's like a tradition, but I wish they would learn another song or two."

"We don't have music except classical where we are," Aurora said quietly. "I wish we did. I heard that once everyone used to sing and that they used to play music on the radio."

Mrs. Xiomy put her fork down and said, "Yes, they used to have a genre per station. It was quite wonderful, fitting everyone's taste. They even had hip-hop, which my husband loved. Poetry with a beat."

Eileen nodded. "There are some people here who can do that. It's quite extraordinary, but I don't think they're performing tonight. Maybe at the next party."

Boreas was watching Babs curiously. He said, "Thanks for the hole in my jacket. You actually made it something I would wear."

She laughed. "Glad you noticed. Would have made it larger but didn't want people to think it was due to my lack of handiwork. I would never get another job down here."

"If they ask, I'll say that I wanted it that way. That's the style from us land folks."

Aurora and Eileen watched them flirting, and Aurora felt a twang of jealousy in her chest. Eileen tugged at her and said hurriedly, "I want to introduce you to someone. He's so cute and has been asking about you."

Aurora felt uneasy about leaving Boreas and Babs together but couldn't deny Eileen this. It was like having a friend again, like having Mary again. She followed Eileen across the dance floor, hand in hand toward a table parallel from them. She turned just in time to see Babs steal her seat and whisper something in Boreas's ear. She didn't know why she was getting this sick reaction and quickly drove it from her mind as they approached a young man of about sixteen who was sitting at the table.

"Roland, this is my friend Aurora."

He rose and was around the same height as Aurora. He was dressed in elegant attire with a red bowtie, and he kissed her hand.

"You are very beautiful. May I have this dance?"

She turned to Eileen who looked so excited and urged her on with her hand. Aurora gave her assent, and as he led her to the dance floor, she admired his defined arm muscles. He looked like he could pick her up and not worry that she had eaten a full dinner and extra rolls. The song started, and he put his arms around her waist, touching his face against her own. He smelled like garlic and rose petals, and she tried not to cough as they started to dance. She ended up stepping on his toes more than once, but he pretended not to notice as they continued to dance around the room.

"So how do you like it down here?" he asked to make conversation.

"It's really beautiful," she said truthfully. "I have never seen or heard of anything like it."

"My father helped design it along with the High Magistrate. Quite remarkable infrastructure, similar to a submarine with plexiglas windows and depressurized compartments. They use an oxygen generator, where through the electrolysis of water, the water is converted into oxygen. The carbon dioxide that we exhume is released back into the ocean. And they have dehumidifiers spaced throughout the rooms to prevent moisture from condensing on our walls. This process keeps us all able to breathe like normal. Quite remarkable."

"And the elevator idea?"

"Ingenious. Of course you've ridden in it. A man helped design it from the land above. He was asked to live down here but refused. Said he needed to disappear."

"Do you know his name?"

"Professor Gassendi."

She stomped on his foot in shock and quickly jumped off it. "Professor Gassendi. The Gassendi heir! Do you know where he is?"

"No." Roland winced, rubbing his foot trying to disguise the anguish in his voice. "No, but the High Magistrate does."

He whirled her around, and her eyes haphazardly fell over to her table where she noticed two empty seats, and she felt bitter saltiness as she tried to swallow. So Boreas fell for engaged women. Why would that surprise her? She turned to the orchestra, where Babs's fiancé was warming up his vocals to prepare for his song, unaware that his soon-to-be wife was off gallivanting with Boreas. She wondered what this man would do about it.

"How is marriage down here?" she asked, and Roland nearly tripped over his feet at the question.

"Why, it is the same as up there, except we do religious ceremonies, of course. But the main purpose to the marriage is to procreate to keep this colony strong. Most young women from sixteen to eighteen have arranged marriages. My parents are still arranging mine, and you are of eligible age."

Aurora stepped away from Roland, thanking him for the offer but stating matter-of-factly that she was not going to be staying in the country for long. She hurriedly made her way back to the table and wondered if that was Babs's game, to get out of her arranged marriage. Or maybe she was going to trick Boreas into staying down with her for as long as she could. As she said, no one left Plymouth Tartarus. Perhaps she wanted it that way.

"She is not going to ruin our mission," Aurora thought madly. She ran up to Mrs. Xiomy and demanded, "Do you know where they went?"

"Oh, kids just having fun. I saw you dancing with that nice-looking boy. What's his name? Does he have an older and attractive father, preferably single with no drama?"

Aurora marched over to Otus and tugged at his pant leg to get his attention from the group of children asking for his autograph.

"Have you seen Boreas?"

"Why? Is he in trouble?"

She sighed deeply. What was she doing? She was not Boreas's keeper. Why did she care where he went?

Otus patted her on the head. "Relax and have fun. He'll show up."

She grabbed a glass of water and chugged it down. It helped calm her nerves a bit. She then found Eileen, and together they danced as Babs's fiancé sang their two songs. They were absolutely horrendous. No wonder Babs wanted them to learn different songs. She turned to Eileen and asked, "Are you having an arranged marriage too?"

She shrugged. "Unless I find someone I am in love with first. But all the boys here are so immature. I hope that I'll have another visitor come down to us before my parents have to make a decision."

"What if you want to stay single? What if you don't want to get married?"

She turned to her as if she had three heads. "Why would I not want to get married?"

Aurora took a step back and shrugged. "I mean, women have careers. Some never get married. Others have children and never marry; freezing their eggs so that they can have children in their forties. But then again, it's a different world up there."

"A strange world," Eileen said. After another dance she turned to Aurora. "I never thought of having—what do you call it?—a career. What kind of career do you want?"

Aurora smiled. "Well, I first want to go to college and possibly study history. Then I could go for teaching and help mentor other children. But the history I would love to teach is no longer in the curriculum. We can only teach everything starting with the Last Straw Protest."

Eileen nodded along with the music, and they continued to dance. A bunch of boys joined them, and she started dancing from one to the other. This was the best night of her life, having so many people admiring her, and she continued dancing and dancing until out of nowhere a loud booming noise erupted over the intercom, and everyone froze in place.

Eileen clung to Aurora's arm, worried. "Oh my god!" she said, her face turning pale.

"What is that noise?" Aurora asked, alarmed.

The doors swung open, and Boreas was led into the room by two cloaked figures, an electrical cord bound around his wrists.

Chapter 13

The Confrontation

Boreas was shoved down onto his knees in the center of the ballroom, followed by Babs, who was led out by two other cloaked men. Fawn stood up, horrified, and everyone else looked on with blank expressions. Aurora took a step back to the edge of the dance floor, holding onto Eileen, who looked as if she might fall over at any minute.

Fawn spoke out. "What is the reason for disturbing the party?"

The Great Secretary stepped forward. "We found the accused kissing Miss Barbara O'Hara in the Sacristy, amidst the sacred books!"

The audience cried out in confusion and anger. Babs's fiancé stepped forward, his face filled with anguish.

"Babs, is this true?"

She started to sob uncontrollably, and Boreas was flung to the ground.

The fiancé continued, exasperated, "He's an agitator. He must have forced himself onto her. Justice must be served!"

"No! No, he didn't," Babs cried out. "Please. It's all my fault."

"Silence!" Fawn's voice boomed out, and everyone went silent.

Boreas hadn't said a word, and Aurora caught his eye, but he immediately looked the other way. Otus was standing, unsure of how to proceed. Mrs. Xiomy held his arm, and everyone appeared to be waiting for Fawn to pass sentencing.

"Do you have anything to say for yourself?" she asked, pointing down at Boreas, who finally looked up and stared at her square in the face.

"I have nothing to say to you," he said brusquely, and the armed guards shocked him with an electric current that flowed through the electrical cord. His body shook in convulsions.

"Speak in your defense, or else I will have to sentence you. And our laws down here are not the same as what you have in Candlewick, Boreas."

"You have no right to call me by my name."

"Who do you think gave you your name?"

"A mother doesn't abandon her child at five years old for this place!"

The Great Secretary ordered the guards to shock him again but this time Fawn cried out, "Stop! Take him to the chapel. Both of them! The party will continue despite this momentary disturbance."

The officers lead Boreas and Babs away, and Fawn followed suit with the Great Secretary at her heels. The band started up the music, but Aurora grabbed Eileen's hand. "Come on!"

They snuck out after the group as the rest of the congregation proceeded with talking and dancing. She turned to Eileen. "Do you know a way that we can eavesdrop? A secret chamber? Anything?"

"There's the vent," she said, snapping out of her stupor. "I used to have to clean there when I was younger."

Aurora followed Eileen as they headed to a picture, which she removed to reveal a grated vent. She unlocked it, and together they clambered inside, replacing the vent behind them. They then crawled through the narrow, dark passageway. Aurora felt like a mouse crawling unobserved through the walls. She couldn't see anything in front of her but followed Eileen's movements until they got to a place light was emanating from slits in the vent. They both put their ears against it and listened to the conversation echoing from below.

"You are going to be locked up for a long time! Kissing a woman who is already betrothed is punishable by ten years in prison."

"My fiancé has the right to not press charges!" Babs cried out vehemently. "And he never wanted to marry me. Our parents are forcing us!"

"So you thought doing this would get you out of it. Is that it?" Fawn's voice fired out. Babs grew silent. Aurora saw her head over to Boreas, who was on his knees, the guards directly behind him, his hands still held behind his back by the electrical cord.

"And you, making a scene in the Great Hall. I am the High Magistrate. Just because I gave birth to you, don't think that I won't adhere to the laws."

Eileen turned to Aurora in shock, but Aurora didn't pay attention. She was trying to come up with a way to save Boreas from his fate. If his mother wouldn't intervene for him, no one would.

"Why don't you take your medieval laws and shove them up your ass," Boreas exclaimed. "You're probably glad that this happened so that your secret won't reach Dad or Jonathan. Do you remember them? Huh? Or have you chosen this other family, your new family!"

"Leave us!" she ordered. The guards dragged Babs out, and she cried out to Boreas to forgive her. The doors slammed shut, and it was only Fawn, the Great Secretary and Boreas in the room. She went over to him, put her hand under his chin, and raised his face to hers.

"There has not been a day I haven't thought about you, what I gave up. But I had to, and I couldn't drag you and your brother down with me. Your father never would have allowed it. To die was the only way that I could disappear and be forgotten and yet forgiven. You have to understand that."

He continued to stare into her eyes and said slowly, "Just because I'm your son doesn't mean I have to forgive you. I hope your sacrifice was worth it because you are dead to me. You will always be dead to me. Because to think of you in any other way breaks my heart! I'm just your visitor. A freaking visitor!"

She released her hold on him, and he bent his head down like a wounded animal. Then she rose to her feet turning her back on her son. "Great Secretary, what is the ruling?"

"For the girl, she is to go through with the marriage if her fiancé will still take her. But she will have no privileges of marriage and will continue to have to serve in addition to give birth. For Boreas Stockington, five years in intensive religious service, and he will remain incarcerated until his years are up."

Aurora shook her head and immediately started to unfasten the grate. "Eileen, get out of here," she ordered as she lifted the vent cover upwards to expose a square opening in the ceiling. Eileen scampered off without another word, and Aurora reached out to grab the edge of the velvet curtain. She couldn't believe she was doing this but closed her eyes tight and wrapped her legs around the fabric. She slid down the curtain, landing on her feet just behind the throne. Boreas, having seen Aurora perform her circus stunt, quickly cried out to Fawn to distract her from turning around. "You got what you wanted, huh? You got to keep me here as a prisoner. To keep me from Dad and from Jonathan!"

"You chose to break the rules of our land!"

"You know perfectly well I didn't know I was breaking anything! But I'm glad I kissed that girl! I would do it all over again even knowing the rules because you know what? I am a rule breaker. Always have been. I give Dad a lot of hell back home. And don't think I'm going to be quiet while serving the religious orders either."

The Great Secretary took out a long sharp bladed knife and held it up to his face, yanking Boreas's hair until his head was pointed upward. "I will cut out your tongue, you insolent boy. She is the High Magistrate and you will pay her your respect!"

Aurora spotted the sparkling silver gun on a pillow beside the throne and grabbed it instinctively. Before she had time to be frightened, she jumped out from behind the throne with the gun raised.

"You touch his tongue, I swear I will shoot your High Magistrate in the head!"

Fawn whirled around, and the Great Secretary didn't flinch, still holding onto Boreas's hair.

"Of course, there are times that he won't shut up, so maybe losing his tongue wouldn't be so bad."

"Aurora, you aren't helping!" Boreas exclaimed.

"Oh, I mean, release him or else I'll shoot," she threatened with her finger on the trigger. Aurora had never fired a gun in her life, and she hoped she was holding it correctly. She was envisioning how the guards did it back in Candlewick Prison and hoped she was impersonating them correctly. She opened the safety and held the trigger with her pointer finger, trying hard not to appear nervous though her hand was shaking.

The Great Secretary laughed and exclaimed, "She couldn't shoot you even if she tried, High Magistrate. Let me complete this job, and then we'll take care of the girl together."

Fawn stared at Boreas, the knife inches away from his throat, and she then pivoted back toward Aurora. "What do you want?" she demanded. The Great Secretary looked on, horrified, as she was negotiating with the armed girl.

"Let Boreas go, and release him from his sentence immediately!"

The High Magistrate nodded her consent. "Done! Great Secretary, let him go!"

He shook his head, the knife now at the cleft of Boreas's chin. "I will not let you give in to them. Once you waver in your sentencing, people will not adhere to you. We cannot risk error. We cannot risk them to turn against you!"

"Or what? We will end up exactly like the people we are fighting against. Have we become the Common Good? Are we just as twisted as they are?'

"You're blinded because he's your son, High Magistrate! You know you cannot back down from this. You have a duty to your people. She cannot shoot you. She doesn't know how to kill! She's a girl, for heaven's sake!"

"If you hurt him, I swear I will hit you square in the heart!" Aurora declared, taking a step down from the altar and pointing the gun in the direction of the Great Secretary.

The Great Secretary looked to the High Magistrate for assistance, but none was given.

"Put down the knife, Great Secretary."

"I cannot let you do this!" he yelled madly, his pupils glaring, and he sliced the knife across Boreas's neck, slitting his throat. The Great Secretary lifted the bloody knife up as if to strike again when a shot fired, the bullet hit him right in the center of his forehead. His body jolted and then fell backwards onto the ground, blood oozing down his face. Aurora stared down at her gun, but no bullet had been fired. Her finger was still resting on the trigger. Smoke instead was emanating from under Fawn's cape.

Fawn dropped the gun and ran to Boreas, who was bleeding heavily by the neck.

"Quick, Aurora, run out and tell the guards to fetch the doctor. Now!"

Aurora ran down the steps and yelled at the first guard she spotted outside the door to quickly find the doctor. She then ran back to where Fawn held Boreas in her arms, blood seeping into her clothing. She had ripped part of her cloak and was using it to try to stop the bleeding, applying pressure to the wound. Boreas looked as if he was about to go into shock, his face pale and his eyes rolled to the back of his head.

"It looks like it just missed the main jugular artery. We need to act quickly. Get some alcohol from the inner cabinet."

Aurora ran to the cabinet, fetched the bottle, and handed it back to Fawn, who poured it onto the wound to ease the infection. Boreas winced in pain, not able to speak. She rocked him in her arms, and Aurora knelt down beside them, helping to hold Boreas's hand while Fawn's soothing voice whispered, "Hang on, Boreas. Help is coming."

The doctor appeared in the doorway and ran to the patient and told Aurora to leave and wait for them outside. She obeyed and the doors slammed shut behind her. She stood gaping at the door, not knowing what to do. She ran back to the Great Hall, blood soaked into her maroon dress. She had to find Otus. He would know what to do. He was still at the table waiting for her. When he saw her in the doorway he immediately got up and gave some excuse to the table, with Mrs. Xiomy following his lead.

Aurora was in a state of shock and Otus picked her up, asking, "What is it? What happened?"

As they walked to the Sanctuary, Aurora relayed the events of the past half hour to Otus.

"There's nothing we can do but wait," she said. "Oh, Otus, what are we going to do?"

He shook his head, worried. "I should have listened to him. We should have left before the gala! We should never have abandoned our mission at hand."

She dug her face into his tuxedo sleeve, and he carried her back to the Sanctuary. She changed out of her blood-soaked clothes and into her shirt and jeans while Otus went to see to see if there was any news yet on Boreas's fate.

Mrs. Xiomy put her arm around the young girl and held her tightly. "He's a survivor. Like we both are. He'll get through this," she said.

"I didn't even react. I didn't expect the Great Secretary to go through with it. I didn't know that he would slit his throat, and I just stood there with the gun pointing and nothing happened. I failed Boreas."

"It's not easy to kill. Fawn did one right thing by her son. Boreas is in his mother's hands now."

Aurora watched as Mrs. Xiomy drifted off to sleep. She snuck out of the room and entered the Sacristy with the great books lined up and illuminated with a solitary light. She got down on her knees as she saw the others do earlier that day. She folded her hands and prayed to a god up above, if one did exist, to watch over Boreas.

"Please let him get well," she whispered. She found the words comforting to say, and she kept repeating them over and over again, thinking that if anyone or anything could cure Boreas, it was a god. She continued to pray over and over again until darkness swept over her.

Chapter 14

The Oubliette

urora awoke to find herself in her bed in the Sanctuary. The events of the night before played over and over again in her mind like a nightmare. She turned to see that she was alone in the room. She got up and opened the door. Nobody was there, and she dreaded the worst. Why didn't anyone wake her up? Unless Boreas didn't make it.

She ran down the hall and to the Sacristy. She nearly ran smack into Eileen, who was carrying the breakfast tray.

"Eileen! Where is he? Is he...?"

"He's alive! I thought someone had told you by now!"

Aurora didn't let her finish. She threw her arms around her friend and hugged her so tight that she dropped the breakfast tray onto the floor.

"Where is he? Is Otus with him? I need to go to him."

Eileen showed her the way to another chamber that they hadn't been allowed access the day before. She didn't bother to knock and opened the door wildly, stepping forth into a grand bedroom with bookshelves lining each of the four walls. There was an open ceiling letting in an ominous blue-gray light and there were candles lit on each of the four walls. A large canopied bed stood at the center of the room, and there sleeping on the bed with a thick bandage around his neck was Boreas. Otus was standing over him, bending down slightly and holding his hand tenderly. Mrs. Xiomy was busy talking to the doctor in the corner. His features she hadn't cared to notice the night before, but he was an attractive man with a mustache and thick graying brown hair. He wore glasses with small clear lenses and was writing something vigorously on a pad of paper. Fawn was nowhere to be found.

She ran to the bedside and Otus put his hand up to indicate a whisper. "He's asleep, but he's a fighter this one. I told you my first impression was right. The doctor said he'll make a full recovery."

"He shouldn't be moved until tomorrow," The doctor added ripping a sheet of paper from the pad and handing it to Mrs. Xiomy. "He's lost a lot of blood, and rest is the best thing for him now."

Aurora sat on the edge of the bed and gazed down at Boreas, who was asleep, cleaned up from the night before. She continued to experience flashbacks of him bleeding to death in his mother's arms.

"I am glad he's okay," she said, finding the words hard to say as she took his hand in her own.

The doctor exited, and Mrs. Xiomy thanked him again for all that he did. When the door had closed shut behind them, Aurora turned to Otus and angrily snapped, "Why didn't you wake me up?"

Otus continued to hold Boreas's hand. "You had a rough night too. I thought it best that you sleep. There was nothing else you could have done. I carried you back to your room once I heard the doctor's report."

"Yeah, you still should have woken me when I was in the Sacristy."

"Praying?" Mrs. Xiomy said putting her hand on her shoulder.

Aurora fumbled with her shirt sleeves, annoyed she had gotten caught. "Figured it did no harm to try."

"Which god did you pray to?"

"The one that would help Boreas." She obstinately clenched Boreas's hand a little tighter, afraid that he would slip away from her again, like he nearly did the night before.

Suddenly his eyes flickered open and adjusted to the light trying to make sense as to where he was. He opened his mouth and tried to speak, but Mrs. Xiomy stopped him, "Don't try to speak. It will take a few days for the wound to heal. But you're going to be okay. We're all here."

His eyes perused over them from face to face until he stopped on Aurora and didn't take them off her. He took her palm in his hand and using his fingernail, gently wrote the words *I'm sorry* against her skin.

"Stop it," she said choking back tears. "You just get better, okay? And no more kissing other women, you got that? I don't want to have to swing down the curtains like Tarzan again."

The door swung open and in walked Fawn, looking frail with dark circles under her eyes. She was carrying some medicine with her. "I had them ground this up for him this morning. An herbal remedy my mother used to make me."

Aurora stood up to allow room for Fawn to get close to her son. She gently touched his forehead and then his cheek with the back of her hand. Then she mixed the medicine with a glass of water, and then fed it to him through a straw. He grimaced in pain as he swallowed but no longer did he glare at Fawn like a stranger. He stared at her like a boy gazing into the eyes of his mother.

"It was a close one, but you'll make it. My son doesn't go down without a fight. It will take more than a knife to defeat him."

Aurora then turned to Fawn, knowing that it was now or never to approach her about their mission. She deserved the right to know.

"Fawn, I am sure Boreas would tell you this if he could, so I will tell you for the both of us."

She sat up stiffly and faced Aurora.

"Boreas and I are on a mission to help Otus get to the northern lights. We are fulfilling a prophecy that we need to be there together in order to save the planet from a Geometric Storm. The prophecy is based on a book that is now in the possession of the long-lost heir of Pierre Gassendi. I was told last night that the heir had helped to design the glass elevators but had decided to stay on the mainland. Do you know where we can find him?"

She stood up and paced the room back and forth. "You and Boreas are on this mission? No, it is not true. When he said it I didn't believe it."

"You mean David's prophecy, before he died."

Fawn stared at Mrs. Xiomy, her expression changing to hatred. "Are you trying to get back at me? Getting my child involved in this wild goose hunt. This suicide mission! I nearly lost him last night. He is not getting mixed up with you again."

"It's his choice. They approached me, mind you," Mrs. Xiomy declared defensively.

"And they answered the conch shell." Otus added.

Fawn stood up and fixed the sheets over her son's chest, her matronly instincts coming back at full force—to protect her son at any cost. She pulled back the hood of her cloak, and her hair was a wavy mess that was tangled down her back. It caused her to look more like Medusa than the goddess she appeared the day before.

She pointed at Mrs. Xiomy and exclaimed, "It is because of you that we are even down here. You turned your back on the rebellion, gave us all up like pigs to the slaughter, to save a man who didn't want any saving!"

"I am sorry!" Mrs. Xiomy gasped. "I will never forgive myself for what I did. But I loved David. What would you have done, Fawn?"

"You know what I would have done!" she snapped back. "And I hope wherever he is he knows what a coward you became at the end. Still a coward! Hiding away on Wishbone Avenue in that house of yours, afraid of the world and everyone in it. Don't now use my son and this girl to fight this battle for you."

She had been leaning toward her, Fawn's mouth like a viper snapping out words that had been repressed for fifteen years. Mrs. Xiomy's back was against a wall. There was no trace of the rebellious woman with the scarf that Aurora had witnessed back on Wishbone Avenue. It was as if that courageous act of fearlessness was a fleeting glimpse of the woman from her past; replaced with one who had felt loss and could never go back.

"You're right," Mrs. Xiomy replied. "I am a coward. I was also a woman in love. And I can't deny that I thought what David said was a man's illusion on his deathbed. But you cannot deny that the Aurora Borealis is true! And the giant exists! How can you deny that this is their destiny and we are now a part of it, whether we want it or not? We either end it here or we keep moving toward the lights."

Fawn stepped back into the shadows, her eyes illuminated by a solitary candle flame. She looked from Otus to Aurora, and finally her eyes rested on Boreas, who was now fully awake. He was making a motion with his finger and Aurora realized he wanted to write something. She saw the pad and pen that the doctor had been using to write on and quickly handed it to him. He scribbled something nearly illegible, but Aurora handed it to Fawn, who took it and read it.

She immediately crumpled it into her palm and left the room, the door slammed shut behind her.

Otus turned to Aurora. "What did he write?"

Aurora looked down at Boreas who had once again fallen under the spell of sleep. She picked up the crumpled piece of paper and opened it with her fingers.

It read: *Please Mom*.

✵ ✵ ✵

The burial of the Great Secretary happened that afternoon, and Aurora, Otus, and Mrs. Xiomy were all in attendance, despite the conflict in their hearts that the man tried to kill their friend. Fawn presided over it and had informed the country that his death was due to self-defense, that he had gone mad in his final hour. The people still congregated to pay their respects. There were multiple religious services happening simultaneously. Aurora couldn't comprehend how these people with all different beliefs were able to worship freely with no fighting. How were they able to live under the same roof?

Eileen said that this had not always been the case. Before the IDEAL took power, there was a war, with each sector fighting against each other: Muslim against Muslim, Catholic against Catholic. It was the Civil War of Religions that soon grew until it was meant to wipe out everyone from the opposite religious factions. It got so bad that friend fought against friend and family member against family member. Something needed to be done.

That was when the IDEAL came out with his political platform. The idea of abolishing religion across the world was to create unity amongst the people and prevent humankind from killing each other over something that no one had been able to prove existed. The IDEAL gathered followers, and eventually the wars started ending on their own as religious sectors realized they had to band together or else everything their people had fought and died for was for nothing. Without religion, they were going to lose their way of life and their belief structure. Soon all the religious protestors stood tall together to fight under David Xiomy, who led their rebellion and told everyone that though they may disagree on a lot of things, they all believed in something, and that meant everyone was fighting for the same cause. It took someone like him to make people wake up and realize their petty differences were causing hate, which was something every religion was against.

A bronze statue of David Xiomy stood in the center of the Great Hall, his back to the people, just like the picture of him of being taken away by the guards. Though he was being taken away to be killed, he was still fighting for what he believed in. That gave the people hope.

"No wonder he had two women fighting over him," Aurora thought, admiring this man who was able to do so much in such a short amount of time. She wondered what his face looked like, but no one had a picture. They were all destroyed in the hope of destroying his legacy. They could not prevent people from spreading the story. They could control the Internet, the phones, and the satellites, but they couldn't prevent people from telling stories, and the story spread from mouth to mouth to mouth. Eventually that was how this country was formed, this rebellion on the bottom of the ocean floor.

Aurora rode the glass elevator to the meditation center, also known as the Oubliette, the place of forgetting. She felt she needed to get away from everyone and take a moment to breathe and figure out what they were going to do next. She stepped out of the elevator and into a hexagonal glass structure. The elevator retreated back to the main building, and Aurora felt like she was suspended in the water, surrounded by a hexagon of glass; the sides and even the floor and ceiling were made of glass, so it was almost as if she was sitting in the center of the ocean. She peered out in all directions as beautiful species of fish and sea life floated past her, curious of this unknown species inhabiting their space. Who was she, and what was her purpose there? Was she friend or foe? Aurora contemplated these thoughts over and over again, watching amazing species of fish swim up to her and look into her eyes, contemplating if each of these beings had a soul. Did one hand control all of these things, all of life's events? Was someone controlling where she was right now or did they have free will to speak out against their fate and start a new path?

She was trying to piece together the pieces of this puzzle. She now understood how Boreas was involved on this mission, being Fawn's son, but what was her purpose? She was in the epicenter of this mission to save mankind, and she just sat there looking out and contemplating, "Why me? Why was I chosen for this?"

She sat on the glass, looking down into the ocean and spotting snails, turtles, and coral. She was aware that though not visible to the naked eye, microorganisms also inhabited this space. Though she couldn't see them, she knew they were there. Could there be a soul? Something that made her unique, special compared to the others on this planet? There must have been a reason she could hear the conch shell. Could there be something more inside her that she didn't see herself?

The fish darted away as if sensing a danger in the ocean. She stood up slowly and peered out into the ocean, but there was no sign of a shark or other dangerous wildlife. Her eyes darted upward, where she spotted a large fish blocking the sun from streaming down into the ocean. It all went dark, except for a small glow of light from the Oubliette. Her body started pumping adrenaline as it recognized danger, and she quickly pressed for the elevator to return to her, hitting it multiple times and realizing it was not coming fast enough.

Just then something dropped from the large gray outline and sunk toward her. It floated down like a weight and exploded into the ocean. The floor and the walls around her shook violently and caused a slight crack in the glass. Air was immediately compromised, and she held her breath as water started to seep into the hexagon. She would only have a minute until she ran out of air, and she pressed the button again more urgently as another explosion rocked her and the glass below her cracked. She immediately jumped to the other side as it went crashing under due to the extra weight. Another crack was forming where she was standing, and water was seeping in, now at her waistline. Who was attacking them? How did they know where to find her?

The door swung open, and she jumped into the glass elevator as the doors shut just in the nick of time and the water drained from the grates. The elevator went soaring through the ocean back to the main building of Plymouth Tartarus. As soon as the doors swung open, she cried out, "We are under attack!"

Immediately the red alarm was raised, and everyone in the Great Hall started to follow their emergency protocol. Fawn was there on the intercom, having also seen the attacks on her sonar radar, and informed everyone to remain calm and follow what they had practiced. Everyone was to get to their designated submarine and to head to the safe haven immediately.

Aurora crashed into people swarming madly past her. She ran to Fawn and exclaimed, "What about us? Where should we go?"

"You will come with me on Submarine 1. Otus, I am afraid, is on his own. There is no submarine large enough to fit him."

"What about the glass elevator. It is large enough for him. It brought him down here!"

Fawn shook her head. "Otus cannot return to the cave. I am sure that is how they have located us. I am sure he would rather risk death than be taken by the Inspector. I am sorry."

She hurriedly announced more instructions over the intercom, instructing the mission control team to attack the ship that was dropping the bombs. "Take it out of the water," she ordered, and the torpedoes were released, soaring through the water. However, more bombs exploded close to their proximity. They must have deployed the air force in their general direction. Though not able to be seen, the Common Good knew they were down there. And that made it even more deadly.

Aurora ran like mad toward the Sanctuary where she found Otus and Mrs. Xiomy. They had her backpack with them and were on their way to get Boreas.

"Otus, we are under attack. I think they found out we were here. We have to get you out of here now!"

"Not without Boreas!"

"He is going to be with his mother in Submarine 1. Mrs. Xiomy, go with him and make sure he gets there safely."

"What about you, Aurora?"

"We are hijacking the elevator. It's the only thing large enough for Otus."

Otus turned to her and smiled. "I have some tricks up my sleeve too, Aurora. You have seen how fast I can run. I can swim fast too!"

Aurora looked at him, astonished. "And you can hold your breath?"

"I think I'll be able to manage. You get into that submarine with Fawn and get the answers we need before we lose her too. If she plays some 'go down with her ship' nonsense, then we are all lost."

The floor shook under them, and water started to seep through the glass walls. She dashed to the bedroom, where Boreas was struggling to get onto his feet. Otus lifted him up carefully into his arms, and Boreas whispered, "What's happening?"

"They found us!" Aurora cried back, and they made their way through the hall toward the south wing, which held the submarines. They ran into Babs, who was searching for Eileen. Alarmed, Aurora agreed to search with her, but Mrs. Xiomy grabbed her by the arm, insistent that they continue to head for the submarines.

"This place is not going to hold, Aurora. I mean, it's made out of glass, for heaven's sake!"

"I have to find Eileen! Just go!"

They separated and Aurora, along with Babs, ran up and down the halls, banging into people left and right as they searched for any sign of Eileen's red hair. Fawn's voice was still sounding instructions through the loudspeaker, and water was gushing in through cracks in the wall. They passed the Sistine Chapel and saw some of the workers trying desperately to salvage some of the panels as others were covered with water, the paint streaming down the old man's face like tears in the center panel. As they were passing the Sacristy, Aurora caught a glimpse of Eileen's red hair nearly hidden by a fallen plank. She ran to it with Babs by her side, and they lifted the heavy plank off her. Eileen had a huge gash across her eye, and the plank appeared to have crushed her rib cage. She was barely breathing, and Aurora looked at Babs, knowing there was no way they could move her.

"Eileen! Oh my god." Babs hugged her sister and kissed her gently on the forehead. "Oh God, please help us!"

Eileen shook her head, gasping for breath. "Please don't worry about me."

Babs shook her head furiously. "No, I will not leave you!"

Eileen blinked her eyes fighting back tears. "You must leave. Both of you."

Aurora kissed her friend on the forehead, and a tear slid down her face. She tried to hide the fear in her voice. "I will make sure your sister gets to the safe haven. But you are coming with us too, Eileen. You are coming too!"

Eileen tried to shake her head, but she couldn't. "I am going to God's house now. He will take care of me."

The water was now gushing into the Sacristy. Hooded figures were working tirelessly to get the books out of their glass cages, not noticing the three young women huddled in the corner. Eileen grabbed Babs's hand and gave it another squeeze. The golden cross necklace was clutched in her palm and she held it out toward Aurora, the last movement she was able to make. Aurora took it and kissed her hand, taking the cross from her friend.

"God be with you." Eileen said with her final breath.

Babs shook her sister, trying to wake her up, as the water covered her body like a blanket. She started screaming in hysterics as the glass ceiling shattered from another explosion, and Aurora grabbed Babs and pulled her away, grasping the cross tightly in the palm of her hand. She spotted Fawn giving orders in the Great Hall. The windows were exploding, shards of glass sprinkling like rain as people started to scream. Water gushed in toward the high altar in all directions. She remembered Otus's warning. She instructed Babs to keep running toward the submarines and to find Otus. Babs nodded, realizing the gravity of their situation, and took off toward the submarines. Aurora put the cross around her neck and then ran into the main hallway toward Fawn, who was helping an elderly man and woman get to their boats.

"Fawn, you have to leave here now. The rest of the windows are going to break any minute."

Another bomb exploded, causing a huge crash around them, and they bent down, protecting their heads, as shards of glass fell around them. A few grazed Aurora's skin. She grabbed Fawn's hand, but she shook her off.

"No. Get out of here Aurora! Protect my son!"

"To protect your son is to leave here! Dying here is not what he needs. It's not what all these people need! Don't be David! Be Fawn, and be their leader!"

The statue of David Xiomy crumbled to the ground, and Fawn's face was frozen as the statue was swallowed under the onslaught of the waves. She then instructed everyone to abandon their post and to head to the submarines immediately. Fawn stepped down from the pulpit, abandoning her own post, and together with Aurora she helped hold up the elderly couple and lead them to the submarines. Otus was there and quickly lifted them in.

"Seal the main doors shut!" she instructed loudly. Otus slammed them shut, preventing the tidal wave from getting through the cavity. There was no time to check for any wounded or survivors.

Fawn relayed the coordinates of the safe haven to Otus and warned him to be careful. "You will need to be faster than us," she told him. "And don't stop if we get hit. You keep going. After all, it is you they are after. We will distract them as much as we can."

"Thank you, High Magistrate," he said, bowing to her, and with one last reassuring glance at Aurora, he took off beneath the water heading toward the pipes that opened up into the ocean waters. Aurora jumped into Submarine 1, which looked like a giant silver whale made of metal with a periscope sticking out of the blowhole. She was followed by Fawn, who latched the door shut behind her and gave the order for them to submerge and be ready for combat.

Aurora huddled in close to Boreas, who looked so weak and frail beside Mrs. Xiomy. Aurora put her hand over his as a comforting gesture, but his eyes revealed what she was thinking. It would be a miracle if they got out of this alive. The ten submarines submerged and followed each other in linear procession through the circular pipes that resembled sewer systems. As soon as they swam through the final threshold, the submarines shot out into open water, splitting off into different directions. Aurora tried to peer out the porthole to get a glimpse of Otus, but he was nowhere to be found. He must have already gotten a head start. The captain was shouting orders over the intercom to the other submarine drivers. One got hit by a fallen bomb, and there were screams that echoed throughout the loud speaker.

"Submarine 5 has been hit. We are going down!"

Then there was stagnant silence. The others submarines were staying on their target. They shot torpedoes out to sink the top layer of Common Good ships that were blocking the surface. Two of the major battleships were sunk as they continued on their mission. The submarines shook from bombs just missing their target, shaking so tumultuously that leaks began sprouting up. Aurora and Mrs. Xiomy immediately attempted to patch up the areas where the water was seeping through, blocking it with duct tape and other supplies they could scavenge. Fawn was resolute on her course, not letting any of the submarines diverge from the plan. She stood up with the captain, shouting commands into the intercom, a little woman with a loud voice who was working on the last ounce of hope that lay within her. She was protecting her fellow countrymen and women the only way she knew how. Aurora turned back once to see the rest of Plymouth Tartarus collapse, glass shattering like icicles that melted from the line of vision, disappearing beneath the bleakness of the ocean. She glanced over at Babs, who was looking out the porthole, her hand resting on the glass pane as if reaching out for another hand that would never hold it again. Aurora nervously stroked the chain of the gold cross that now lay around her neck. She put her face against the window and watched as the last walls of Plymouth Tartarus collapsed, crumbling to the sands beneath it.

"God be with you too, Eileen," she said softly as they continued forward into the murky darkness.

Chapter 15

Safe Haven

nother bomb exploded and rattled the sides of the submarine as Aurora peered out the window, seeing the last remnants of Plymouth Tartarus plummeting toward the ocean floor. The beautiful glass ceiling and aqua marble walls that made up the castle were demolished, and an eerie emptiness took its place in the ocean. Too many people did not make it out alive, and Aurora felt a tear slide down her cheek thinking about Eileen.

Aurora stuffed the cross beneath her shirt, and it bulged out slightly over her heart. She wiped the tear away and turned toward Boreas, who was silent and looking very frail, the bandage still wrapped around his neck. The doctor had warned them not to move him too early, but there was no choice in the matter. It was either move him or he would have been buried underneath the rubble of Plymouth Tartarus.

The submarine sunk deeper into the dark ocean, and another bomb exploded, just missing them. It rattled above their heads, the aftershocks shaking them so that Aurora lost her balance and grabbed a seat next to Boreas. He took her hand and gave it a reassuring squeeze.

"I hope Otus gets through this," he said slowly. The giant was out there avoiding these bombs like the rest of them. Otus had told her he had some tricks up his sleeve, but how was he, a thirty-foot giant, going to avoid these bombs? He was a direct target and didn't have metal protecting his body.

Another leak sprouted above them from the aftershock, and water started shooting into their submarine. Soaked and freezing, Aurora grabbed more duct tape and towels to patch up the leak and prevent the water from squirming through the hole. Fawn shouted out more orders through the intercom, instructing the other submarines to sink lower and to attack at full force.

"Hit them with everything we have! Attack in a fluid motion. There is only one of them. The planes can't hit us down here."

The nine submarines left began to congregate into battle motion. In unison they released their torpedoes, which soared through the ocean like a school of fish and kept their eye on the target. Fawn stared into the periscope, biting her lip as she watched the torpedoes sailing closer and closer to their end target. After what felt like hours, a huge explosion surmounted above them, sounding like rockets going off on the Independence Day of the Last Straw.

"A direct hit!" she cried out, closing the periscope shut and telling the captain to move at full speed toward the safe haven.

"We cannot wait for them to remobilize. Full speed ahead."

Aurora excitedly turned to hug Boreas, but he was already preoccupied with Babs, who had her arms wrapped around his fragile body. Aurora quickly turned away and marched to the front of the submarine, where she hugged Fawn.

"I knew you would get us out of there," she said still in her embrace.

"I am glad one of us did," Fawn replied, fixing her long hair into a ponytail, her forehead soaked with sweat.

Together they surveyed the damage and checked in with the other remaining nine submarines, but all were able to move forward to their destination, which was less than one hour away. They went dead on their transmission to prevent any radio frequency from being picked up, and all were advised to remain silent as they moved still as shadows through the deep waters.

It felt like an eternity, but finally the captain gave the nod that they were approaching their destination, and Fawn checked her compass necklace and gave the thumbs-up to him to proceed with caution. The captain pressed the button, but nothing happened. Instead of going upward, the submarine started to sink downward. The engine was dead. He pressed the button again more forcefully but still nothing happened.

Fawn stared at him and shouted, "Back-up release valve."

She cringed as again nothing happened, and both she and the captain surveyed the damage to their ship, which was on the starboard side. They hadn't been able to get a visual of it until then, and there was no chance for it to be fixed in time before the oxygen ran out. They watched the other submarines float toward the surface, and Aurora felt her hope deplete, knowing that their fate was never to see the sunlight again.

"We are not dead yet," Fawn declared resolutely. She had them flash their light to the other submarine captains, hoping that one of them would come to their rescue. She flashed it again in Morse code: three long flashes, three short flashes, three long flashes. She kept this going for ten minutes, but there was no response from the other submarines that were too focused on getting their own passengers to safety. Aurora turned toward the fifty-plus people stuffed inside

Submarine 1, with mothers clutching their children in their arms as if they could keep all pain and fear out of that circle of love. She watched as the elderly couple kissed tenderly as if it was the last kiss they would share together in this lifetime. Aurora just felt claustrophobic. She had no one to hold or kiss or say good-bye to. She wished she had been brave enough to tell Jonathan that she cared for him. Now she would never know how he felt. She closed her eyes and pictured herself in his strong arms as he whispered that she was the only girl he had ever cared for. She was the one he had loved all along. Then his face faded into pixels, and all that remained was darkness.

Just then there was a rumble that caused the submarine to shift onto its side, everyone colliding against each other as bodies piled and nearly crushed the people on the bottom.

"Another bomb! We've been compromised. Brace yourselves," Fawn yelled. Everyone huddled in the center of the submarine, awaiting the hit that would mean their lives. Aurora felt her head spinning realizing this was it. This was it.

Huddled with eyes shut, Aurora thought each breath would be her last. But two minutes passed and still no explosion.

Fawn slowly lifted her head and hollered, "Then what in god's name was…"

She shrieked as the submarine started to shift from side to side. They were no longer sinking. They were rising to the surface, the light getting brighter and brighter until they splashed out of the water and were once again floating on the ocean waves. Once the boat had stopped shaking, Mrs. Xiomy and Fawn surveyed the injured. Many people were banged up and bleeding, while others were having trouble breathing. Fortunately everyone was still alive. Aurora spun the wheel and opened the hatch of the submarine. Looking down at them was none other than a dripping wet Otus.

"I should have known it was you," Aurora laughed.

"I told you I was a good swimmer." He smiled back. Seaweed was dripping from the top of his head. She helped the others go up the ladder, and Otus assisted them to shore, where the other passengers from the submarines were already setting up camp. They were relieved that their leader was safe. Fawn heartily shook Otus's hand and said that without him they were surely done for.

"It's times like this I'm glad we have a giant on our side."

Otus carried Boreas to the campsite. He was passing in and out of consciousness, the atmospheric pressure changes taking a toll on him, and they found the doctor, who had managed to salvage his medical bag during the evacuation. Aurora watched Babs search each of the submarines for some sign of her fiancé. There was none. She sat in a corner, assisting an elderly couple who were injured during the submarine battle. Aurora went over to her and said, "I am so sorry, Babs."

She applied the bandage and replied tartly, "Eileen would say it's God's will."

"And what do you say?"

Babs glared up at her. She had the same eyes as Eileen, but these were glazed with hate. "I say God's will be damned!"

Aurora left her in her grief and returned to where the community was setting up camp in this mysterious place that they called the safe haven. It was deep within the crevice of the mountains, and there was a water bank where they had floated up but besides that they were surrounded by purple majestic mountains that had pointed peaks jetting out of the clouds. The land was fertile and moist, and there were large oak and maple trees providing shelter and a canopy from the eyes of the skies. It was as if they had taken the submarine back in time to the days of the Native Americans, where Candlewick and civilization seemed a million miles away as they stood on the border of the forest and wilderness.

Fawn took tools and other essential items out of the submarine and passed them out to people strong enough to help set up camp. Some men took axes and went into the forest to chop wood so they could start building shelters. They had to take precautions that if the Inspector was after them, he did not give up so easily. The community was split, with some members chopping wood and others gathering leaves and twigs and making little huts that could withstand a rainstorm and provide protection from wildlife. Some built fires, using the daylight to mask the smoke so they could prepare food for the injured. Aurora helped some of the women gather seeds and plants in the forest, and they showed her which were edible and which to avoid.

"Don't test anything yourself," one woman named Beth said. "Ask first."

They picked dandelions, clovers, plantains and other edible plants that Aurora had never heard of before.

After chopping wood, gathering seeds and fruit, and cooking, all sat down on the ground under the stars and thanked God for their safety and for providing them passage to the safe haven. They blessed the fallen loved ones who had died fighting for freedom. Their lives would continue to live on through the community.

Fawn adorned her shell headdress on top of her head. Her voice rang out, fierce and resolute. "They may have destroyed Plymouth Tartarus, but they cannot destroy our spirit. Here tonight, I christen this ground Plymouth Incarnate."

The others cheered into the night, and all ate the small amount of food distributed throughout the community, so different from the banquet that they had feasted on the night before at the gala. Aurora sat down beside the maple tree and stared into the ocean, her stomach still empty but grateful for being alive. The stars twinkled above her. She could not remember the last time she saw the stars so vivid. She could make out the constellations on that summer day, pointing out the scorpion and Orion's belt. Her father had taught her these constellations from her backyard. He said that tracing the stars made a map so that you would always know where you were. They had sat together playing games of tracing the stars with their fingers as if connecting the dots. They envisioned themselves as sailors to the new world, following the North Star as their only compass. As long as it was in front of them, they knew they were heading in the right direction.

A rustle in the leaves caused Aurora to turn her head in a flash to behold Otus staring up at the stars beside her. "I didn't want to disturb you," he said, sitting down and causing the thick maple leaves to shake, hiding his head from view.

"Without you, Otus, I'd be down at the bottom of the ocean."

"You know I wouldn't let anything happen to you."

Aurora took a deep breath and continued to gaze up at the stars, leaning against a tree trunk. She plucked some grass with her fingers, and the blades trickled through her fingers, soft and smooth to the touch. She had taken all this for granted: the stars, the night. Even herself. All of it could vanish in an instant, like a blade of grass plucked from the earth by her hand.

"Otus, what do you believe in?"

She heard him take a deep breath, letting it out slowly like air circulating through a heater. He wiggled his hairy toes that were resting on the edge of the shoreline. The waves nearly touched, reaching closer and closer with each ebb and tide.

"What I believe is what I'm still trying to find out."

Aurora stood up and stretched her arms over her head. "I guess that is what we are all still trying to find out."

"But I have a hypothesis."

Aurora turned to him and tried to make out his face through the tree branches. She could only make out the leaves rustling and knew that was where he was breathing.

"You have a hypothesis about a belief?" she scoffed. "Science and religion don't mix. That's what the IDEAL says."

"Do you really think the IDEAL has all the answers?"

She knelt down beside the shoreline and washed her calloused hands in the cold liquid, the water sifting through her fingers. Six days ago, her hands had been innocent and naïve about the world around her. How different these hands looked to her now. She was afraid to gaze at herself through the reflection in the water, afraid that she wouldn't recognize the girl staring back at her.

"I think I should check on Boreas." She kicked a rock, and it went soaring through the air and plopped into the ocean. Otus stood up, and together they walked away from that peaceful sanctuary. She glimpsed one last time at the stars up above, and something her father said came back to her.

"Make a wish, Aurora," he had said, holding her tiny hands when she was a little girl hanging onto his neck in a piggyback ride.

"What do I wish for?"

"Anything you want. They can hear you. But you can't tell anyone else your wish or it won't come true."

She had squeezed her eyes really tight and made a wish and then opened them in a flash, expecting the thing she wished for most to manifest out of thin air before her eyes.

"It didn't come true," she said abrasively, upset that her father had lied to her.

"Maybe it will come true in a way you didn't expect."

Aurora laughed thinking about how young she had been to believe that stars made wishes come true. She squeezed her eyes really tight, and then they shot open in a flash like she had done as a little girl. Once again the thing she wished for most didn't manifest out of thin air.

"We'll see if it comes true," she thought to herself, holding her hand over her heart as she followed Otus's large footprints on the graveled path.

Boreas looked disgusted, eating seaweed soup when they entered his tent. He slurped it loudly as the seaweed slithered down his throat. The color had returned to his face, though the bandage still lay wrapped across his neck right above the jugular vein. Aurora was relieved when she heard his voice was back to normal.

"You just missed her," he said as the green soup dripped down his chin.

"Missed who?"

He took another giant bite out of his soup and squirmed as he swallowed. "Fawn."

Aurora nodded, realizing that he was not comfortable calling Fawn his mother yet. "What did she want?"

He put the spoon down so that it clattered against the wooden bowl. "She is going to tell us where to find the heir of Pierre Gassendi. But news flash for you all. He was a priest."

"The heir?"

"No, the philosopher Pierre Gassendi."

Aurora sat down on the edge of the floor and applied more leaves around his body for comfort. "So there is no heir?"

"Well, the last one in his family's bloodline, I suppose. I am guessing when we meet him we'll find out if he's the right guy."

Otus was outside, as he didn't fit into the tent, and Aurora had to repeat everything being said for him to hear.

"Speak louder," Otus cried out, his voice semi-muffled through the canvas.

"I'll tell you after," Aurora screamed back. She then peered around the mid-sized tent, realizing someone was missing. "Where is Mrs. Xiomy? She's been MIA since we landed here."

Boreas nearly choked on the soup. "It is so nice to be rid of her for five minutes! She's been here all afternoon to be close to the doctor. She was pretty much drooling when he was reapplying my bandage. Thankfully he told her I needed to rest, and the two of them went off to bother someone else besides me."

Aurora laughed outright, and Otus poked his head in to find out what was so funny.

"Boreas who was head over heels for Mrs. Xiomy two days ago now is relieved that she is off driving the doctor crazy! How fickle you are with your love choices."

Boreas threw leaves at Aurora, and she threw them back until they had destroyed what was left of the bed.

"Besides, I was not in love with Mrs. Xiomy. She is every boy's teacher crush! Like you don't have a crush back at home?"

Aurora held the leaves up, about to throw them, but her hand froze at the mention of a crush. Her thoughts immediately flew to Jonathan, and the leaves fell from her fingers. She sat back on her hind legs and said, "Crush? Who said I have a crush?"

He stared at her awkwardly. "It was just a rhetorical question."

The tent flap flung open, and Fawn entered, looking exhausted and completely drained after the day's events. She walked into the room and left the flap open. Mrs. Xiomy was beside her, looking crest-fallen, probably at being dragged from the doctor too early. Even after the disastrous day's events, Mrs. Xiomy's hair was still styled perfectly with not a curl out of place. Her purple glasses were still intact on the tip of her scrawny nose, and her orange and indigo ensemble was wrinkle free. The only dirt visible was on the tip of her purple heels.

Fawn stood awkwardly in the tent and asked Boreas, "How was the soup?"

"It didn't kill me."

She clasped her hands together in satisfaction. "Good. I'm glad." She awkwardly shifted her weight back and forth and then she diverted her gaze toward Otus. "So you are looking for the heir to the famous physicist and mathematician Pierre Gassendi. As you assumed, I do know the heir. He designed our glass elevator at the former Plymouth Tartarus. I didn't want to relay this information to you for my own personal reasons," her eyes stole a glance at Boreas but then returned their gaze in Otus's direction, "but Otus, you did save our lives today, and I am eternally grateful."

She held out a yellowed piece of paper that had been folded in the shape of a triangle. She handed it to Aurora, who cautiously opened the flaps of the paper. Inside there were tiny dots sprawled all over the page.

"By connecting the dots they will lead you to Professor Gassendi."

"Sounds too easy," Aurora questioned, raising her eyebrow in suspicion.

"There's one other catch as well. The professor is extremely paranoid and closed off from the world. He will not just take any visitors, especially if he doesn't know them. While working on the glass elevator he only trusted two people. One of those people is me, but as you can see I cannot abandon my community."

"You always know how to choose, don't you?" Boreas muttered under his breath.

Fawn's oval eyes opened wide, and she clasped her fist toward her mouth, biting the edge of her nail. She sat down on the edge of the bed, but Boreas immediately shifted away from her.

"Boreas, I—"

"Stay with your precious community," he snarled at her. "It's your family, after all."

He stood up and stormed out of the tent, the flap sliding back forcefully into place. Crickets filled the empty silence as Boreas's words acted as daggers into Fawn's heart. She pulled her shoulders back and crinkled her nose.

Aurora said slowly, "It'll take time for him to…what I'm trying to say is…"

Fawn's stoic face didn't flinch. "He's my son. Forgiveness doesn't come easy to our family." She stole a glance toward Mrs. Xiomy and stared at her long and hard. Then she continued, "Besides, he has the right to be angry. I just hope one day he'll understand."

Mrs. Xiomy put her hand on her hips, "The day he understands is the day I join your precious community! Fawn, he's your son!"

"Yes, and I made my choice! I don't have to answer to you for my actions. You're the one who probably led the Common Good to our doorstep."

"Don't forget that without us, you and your little community would be buried in the ocean right about now."

"Without you we would never have been found out. We would have been just fine and not here starting over in this wasteland."

The two women continued to argue, and Otus blew on his two fingers, sounding a loud, piercing whistle. The women broke apart like in a wrestling match.

"Can you try to get along for one minute?"

The two women nodded like guilty children toward the giant who had reprimanded them. They turned their backs on each other, and silence filled the room.

Aurora contemplated what Fawn had said and asked, "But who then, if not you, Fawn, will the professor trust?"

Fawn stepped away from Mrs. Xiomy and went to the tent flap, where she made a motion ushering someone over to them. Stepping through the flap was none other than Babs, her face tight as a boxer. A dark, black veil was draped over her long hair, wearing this accessory for the funeral ceremony that would commence that night. Aurora stepped back, trying to hide the shock of seeing that girl, of all people, step through the tent.

Fawn put her arm around Babs. "I have already spoken with her, and she has agreed to accompany you on this part of your journey. She knows the professor, having been his apprentice during the last stage of the elevator development. She was the only other person, besides me, to get close to the professor and earn his trust."

"He will let me speak with him," Babs said assertively.

Aurora took a step forward and said, "I am sorry, but is she in the right state of mind to come with us? I mean, not that we wouldn't be happy to have her come, but this is a dangerous mission, and she just lost two people close to her."

"If coming with you means that we are one step closer to destroying my sister and fiancé's murderers, then I volunteer for this mission rather than having to wait here and do nothing."

Aurora turned to Otus for help, but he ignored her pleading eyes and nodded his approval to have Babs join the team. The flap of the tent opened, and Boreas walked through, now more subdued and not as tense. He was wearing the doctor's long black cloak over his broad shoulders, smelling of iodine and alcohol.

"The funeral is about to begin."

His eyes darted toward Babs, who gave him a slight smile that only Aurora noticed. They quickly filled him in with the details of their journey and that Babs would accompany them to see the professor. He was delighted to have her join them. Together they walked toward the funeral service, but Aurora stayed behind, saying that she wasn't feeling too well and that she would join them shortly. They didn't protest, letting the flap close shut behind them as Aurora sat alone in the darkness.

She closed her eyes and picked up a lone leaf that Boreas had thrown at her earlier. She twirled it in between her fingers and went to put it back onto the bed when she stopped and snuck it into her coat pocket. As a souvenir, she told herself. Nothing more.

Chapter 16

The Aftermath

Aurora listened as Babs's voice filled the night air with song, an Irish tune that caused even the crickets to pause as she sang her song in honor of those perished by the hands of the Common Good. Soft and melodic, her soprano voice lifted high, with the wind carrying it to Aurora's ears, and she felt her body caught up in the trance leading her toward the circle where everyone sang in harmony with her. She sat down in the outskirts of the circle listening as Babs sang her solo, her voice choking up as she got to the part of the song:

> *I pray I'll see your face again*
> *Though I may not know quite when,*
> *I pray you'll know my love is true*
> *May the road I take now lead to you.*

So let us sing in harmony this day
Despite our eyes, yours brown mine gray,
The sun is one that shines above
One heaven, one hell; one life, one love.

Fawn stood up and gave Babs a hug as the circle continued to hum in harmony with the song.

Otus was sitting in the corner, two children sitting on his lap unaware of the turmoil and the grief being experienced by the adults in that circle. They instead played on Otus's knees, chasing each other and smiling warm-hearted smiles. Aurora watched them and thought how precious they were and how she longed to be a child once more. She had crossed the divide, and there was no way to turn back.

She turned to Otus and said, "We need to leave at the Sacred Hour."

He looked at her and carefully picked up the children, placing them back into the arms of their parents. He followed her to the shadows saying, "We don't even know where the professor is. Connecting the dots did not create a map."

Aurora held out the yellowed document and handed it to him. "It is a map. A map leading us straight into the heart of Orion. If we follow the coordinates, I believe they will lead us to him."

He stared at the stars up above in the shape of the mythical hunter Orion and said slowly, "Is Boreas able to do the journey?"

"He has to be. If the Common Good army figures out that we have headed in this direction, then we need to be ahead of them. We need to get to the professor before they do."

Aurora heard laughter escalating from the circle, and there was Boreas with Babs tucked under his arm. He was reciting a story to Mrs. Xiomy and the doctor, who were listening to his amusing tale.

Otus caught Aurora's glare and went over and scooped up Boreas before he had a chance to interject.

"Otus, you can't just do that," he scolded, fumbling in his fist. Otus laughed, watching him struggle and then put him down on a high tree branch so that he had to listen and not get distracted.

"Since you are hanging in there, Aurora says we need to leave tonight."

"During the Sacred Hour," she added, crisscrossing her arms over her chest.

He hung onto the tree branch, trying not to look down at the ground thirty feet below him.

"You know, I am capable of listening on the ground."

"Not when you have a beautiful woman taking up your attention." Otus laughed, poking him in the chest and nearly knocking him off the tree branch.

"She is beautiful, isn't she?" Boreas said, winking at Otus.

Aurora stood there tapping her foot against the ground and wished they could just leave Boreas hanging on that tree branch forever. How did she get stuck on this mission with him of all people? She coughed so that the boys came back down to earth and repeated, "So the Sacred Hour? I am not waiting for you to agree. There's no other way because Otus can't go leaping through the countryside in daylight. I think he is bound to be noticed."

"So we are going to travel through the Sacred Hour each day? We'll never get to the professor at that rate."

Otus picked up Boreas and placed him back down on the ground. "I'll get us there before the sun rises tomorrow."

✡ ✡ ✡

The bodies washed up along the shoreline of Candlewick Harbor.

Inspector Herald walked along the edge of the cave, wrought with rage as he beheld the faces of each sullen-eyed, blue-faced rebel who had been hidden from him and the Common Good army for the past ten years. He just never suspected that they would be underneath his nostrils in an underwater country in the very town that he himself resided. It was an insult that made his face scowl, and he continued taking long strides over the dead, marking each of those drowned faces in his memory as having a personal vendetta against him and everything the IDEAL stood for.

He had given the order for his chief Officers Woolchuck and Pelican to bomb the area beneath Candlewick Park with hopes of luring out any illegal activity transpiring in the depths of the ocean based on his instinct that the giant and his two teenage counterparts were there. Yet each body that he stomped over was a normal sized human, not a thirty-foot giant. And none of the faces that the Inspector peered into were the faces of those two troublesome teenagers Aurora Alvarez and Boreas Stockington. They must have escaped along with the giant and were now once again out there to fulfill the prophecy.

That damned prophecy. The Inspector cringed, thinking that this was nothing compared to what the Geometric Storm would bring. It would bring an even larger death toll than one hundred atomic bombs. Nature's wrath was nearly as disturbing as his own, but the Inspector had no intention of trying to stop this storm from occurring. Quite the opposite since this Geometric Storm would reinforce to the people who followed him and the IDEAL that religion and a higher being were a negative force on their country. The storm would crush any form of rebellion throughout their country and anyone who was beginning to doubt the Common Good's power. This Geometric Storm would force them to understand that the only person they should turn to and have their faith in was the IDEAL. The IDEAL would be the only one to protect them and save them from this horrible natural disaster. So once the Geometric Storm hit and the world was in despair, the Common Good government could rise to inexplicable power. The Common Good would be the largest world power, with everyone turning to them for answers.

Inspector Herald found himself smiling, though it was painful for his facial features to form a smile, as he rested against the edge of the cave, staring into the blood stained ocean, the water lapping against his boots. Executing David Xiomy had been the greatest victory the Inspector had hoped to achieve in annihilating any further rebellions from taking place. As he looked out at the dead bodies along the shoreline, he realized his life had gone in a full circle, and he was not going to let two troublesome teenagers and a giant disrupt his plans. He vowed that he would find them. He vowed that they would not stand in his way.

"Inspector," a deep voice bellowed behind him.

Inspector Herald continued facing the open crevice of the cave and said in his husky tone, "You'd better have good news for me, Officer Woolchuck."

The officer gulped noisily, and Inspector Herald turned around and even in the darkness could make out his Adam's apple bobbing back and forth, intimidated by the presence of the Inspector. He nearly slipped on the rocks but quickly regained his footing on the slippery slope and sputtered, "Henry Stockington and his son Jonathan are waiting for you back at your office just as you requested."

The Inspector wet his lips and opened his eyes, though hidden behind his large dark sunglasses. Though his eyelids were burned, his pupils had not been scorched by the treacherous flames of the fire that had altered his once human appearance. Now he resembled a picture of Dorian Gray, his soul living on the outer layer of his skin.

"I will go to them now."

"What about the bodies, Inspector?"

The Inspector stared out from this angle at the bodies that lined the ocean shore like seals resting after a long journey on the California coast line, being covered gracefully by the waves.

"Burn them," he replied decisively. "We don't want the public seeing this scene at the Awakened Hour."

The Inspector started charging down the slippery slope and fixed the long slate-colored trench coat with its high collar that ran the full length of his six foot seven inch frame. Other officers and media crew quickly hurried out of his way, careful to not look him directly in the eye. He was about to get into his chauffeured limo to take him back to the Candlewick prison when a young black female reporter approached his window and tapped on the glass with her fist. His chauffeur put the limo into drive, but the Inspector told him to wait and rolled the window down a crack.

"Inspector, my name is Analise Jones for Channel Four news and I want the truth about what happened here tonight at Candlewick Park. I am not buying this boat accident incident, and neither will my viewers."

The Inspector eyed the beautiful and rambunctious reporter admirably, the first reporter in fifteen years to dare approach him like this. Of course she would be the last. He gave a nod, and officers Woolchuck and Pelican grabbed the young reporter, threw her against the limo, and handcuffed her. She called out that she had rights and that the public had the right to know. They stuffed her into a Common Good vehicle, and the other reporters and her cameraman stood back behind the yellow line without another peep. Officer Woolchuck approached the limo and said, "I apologize for that disturbance, Inspector. We will execute her immediately."

He thought about the young reporter and her beauty. Maybe he could have a little fun before they disposed of her. After all, it had been a while since he shared the company of a beautiful woman.

"I will see to her myself," he said, his tongue seductively grazing his chipped front tooth. Officer Woolchuck nodded with a slight bow as he closed the window, shutting out any further disturbances from the crowd who couldn't understand the measures he needed to take in order to keep this country from falling through his fingers like sand through a sieve. His chauffeur maneuvered the limo down the dirt road, and they made their way through the crowd and onward toward the Candlewick government building, where Henry Stockington and his oldest son Jonathan were waiting for him. Before he could enjoy himself with that reporter, he still had business at hand. All he had standing in his way were two troublesome teenagers and an oaf of a giant against the entire Common Good army.

"It will end the same way it did before," he swore to himself. "They will lose."

Chapter 17

Mapping Out the Stars

The community of Plymouth Incarnate was fast asleep when Aurora poked her head out of the tent flap. It was pitch dark, with the fire pits extinguished following the funeral services, the scent of burnt embers lingered in the air. She had her backpack on and a sweatshirt snugly fit over her chest. It was cooler up in the mountains, and she was glad she had packed jeans as well. She tied her hair up in a ponytail and tucked Eileen's cross under her shirt. This piece of jewelry felt comforting, as if there was a piece of Eileen still there with her, looking out for her, though that was impossible. Eileen was dead, her body beneath the Atlantic Ocean.

Boreas yawned as he stumbled out of his tent. He was wearing a dark gray jacket and his orange peddler hat that covered his messy hair. The jacket collar covered the bandage around his neck, and

Aurora nearly forgot that it was there for a minute. It was almost as if they were still just meeting up on Wishbone Avenue at the corner stop sign.

"What are you thinking?" he asked in mid-yawn, looking at her puzzled face.

"I was thinking about Wishbone Avenue."

He snickered with a crooked smile. "I wonder what Jonathan and Dad are doing now. Probably getting ready for the baseball championship."

"You would think that, wouldn't you?" She adjusted her backpack over her shoulders. "Do you think we'll ever see it again?"

A cool wind encircled them at that moment and caused them to shudder, realizing that they were floating on the hands of the wind leading them on a journey where the destination was clear but the path unknown. They met each other's gaze, and he smiled.

"If we do see it again, at least we'll see it together."

Aurora smiled back, that thought reassuring, and then they raced each other down toward the sandy shore where Otus was knee deep in the water, busy scooping out fish and throwing them onto the shore. The fish were flapping on the shore in a pile, wiggling on the sand.

"Breakfast," he called out, holding up the fifth fish in his palm. He threw it with ease, and it landed right on top of the pile. Mrs. Xiomy was lighting the fire, standing out like a sore thumb in a deep purple sweater that clashed with her orange jeans.

"Does your whole wardrobe have to be the colors of the Common Good?" Aurora sighed, plopping herself down beside her teacher.

"You know the school's mandated wardrobe. Besides, I make it look good."

Boreas agreed wholeheartedly, sticking a fish on a stick and holding it up over the fire, searing both sides. Babs sprinted toward them, looking fresh-eyed in the morning with her tresses tied up in a long ponytail. Her cheeks were extra rosy from the early morning chill and highlighted the freckles speckled over her face.

"Morning. Fawn wants us to say good-bye before we leave."

Boreas tossed Babs a slimy fish, and she caught it in a one-hand catch. She crouched down next to Boreas, and they seared their fish together. Aurora immediately felt sick to her stomach. She attempted to leave the campfire, but Otus reminded her that this might be the only meal they would eat for a while. Reluctantly, she squatted down beside Babs and cooked her fish, watching it brown on all sides. She cooked Otus's too, and he stuck the whole fish down his throat and sucked the meat off the bones. He lifted the intact fish bones out of his mouth like a sword swallower and then tossed the bones into the ocean. Mrs. Xiomy shook her head at him and scolded him that it would hurt his digestive system and there would be no puking on her as he was running.

They cleaned up and dumped water over the fire, and the smoke encircled them as they stole one last glance at the safe haven. They didn't know if they would ever see it again. Aurora felt her stomach churn and hoped it wasn't the fish getting even with her. She took a deep breath. The scent of the salt water was invigorating and calmed her nerves. They walked as a single unit toward Fawn's tent, and Aurora grabbed Boreas's schoolbag so that he boomeranged back toward her, his ear pressed against her lips.

"Be nice," she whispered.

He didn't respond but kept his head pointed forward toward the tent flap.

Fawn heard them approaching and stepped outside, a flowing white nightgown draped over her slender figure. Her long, silky, black hair was hanging loosely down her shoulders, and she reminded Aurora of one of those angels she had seen painted in Plymouth Tartarus.

"I am not good with good-byes but wanted to wish you all good luck with your journey. Also, you won't be able to find this safe haven again. But if you need it, we will find you."

It was too early in the morning to decode Fawn's cryptic riddle, but Aurora gave her a big hug and thanked her for everything. Babs promised that she would find a way back to her, and Fawn nodded to her as if they both were in on a secret. Otus knelt and bowed to her, and she kissed the giant on his forehead, making him blush.

Mrs. Xiomy held out her hand to Fawn, and she shook it.

"I know David would want us to work together if he was still here," Mrs. Xiomy said, wiping a tear from her eyes. "I mean, he did love the cause more than he could ever love either of us."

Fawn nodded slowly, and then out of nowhere she embraced Mrs. Xiomy.

"Please keep them safe," Fawn whispered into her ear.

"I will."

They released their hold, and the moment passed; the two women resumed their usual stiff attitude toward each other. The others took a step back as Fawn approached Boreas and he clung to his backpack for support as she walked toward him. She took the peddler hat off his head and fixed his hair with the back of her hand.

"So are you just going to disappear again?" he asked, avoiding her gaze. He tried to grab the peddler hat but ended up taking her hand instead. When he realized his mistake it was too late, and she held onto it and squeezed it in her own.

She smiled. "I never disappeared, Boreas. I'm glad now you know that."

She placed a small white conch shell with an orange interior in his palm and closed his fingers over it.

"The Buddhists depicted this sacred conch shell to be one of the eight auspicious symbols. They believe its sound will help to banish evil spirits, stop natural disasters, and scare away dangerous and poisonous creatures. May it give you a voice when you are in need and bring luck to you and your friends on your journey."

He looked down at the conch shell, in awe of this sacred gift sitting in the palm of his hand. He then looked back up into his mother's hazel eyes, the same eyes that he had inherited, and nodded in thanks.

"I'll find you again," he said firmly.

She smiled at her son and said, "You and I were born in the same month. You are an Aquarius like me. Someone said that those under this astrological sign are either meant for great things or madness." She kissed him tenderly on the cheek and whispered, "Sometimes it takes a little madness to fulfill great things."

Then, like a doe, she gracefully walked barefoot toward the ocean, her feet leaving imprints in the sand. Boreas stood there clutching the conch shell in his hand and took a step toward Otus. He nodded to him, ready to begin the journey. Otus lifted the travelers into his overall pockets, and Boreas stole one last look at his mother; she was facing the ocean and the mountain backdrop beyond, looking out toward the other side of the mountains where they were heading.

Otus took a giant leap into the air, and they took off faster than lightning as the Sacred Hour had struck. They followed the map toward the heart of Orion, which was depicted clearly in the night sky. They flew over mountains. One giant leap from Otus resulted in ten miles, and he flew with each giant step he took. The wind was icy cold as they soared through the atmosphere, and Aurora told Babs to hold on tighter as she clutched the fabric, too terrified to scream.

Aurora screamed, "Woohoo!" into the night sky, knowing that they were the only ones awake during this Sacred Hour. But that wasn't true, as she realized the mountains and the valleys were awake and embracing the night and the incoming breath of dawn.

Otus lunged over the lush green valleys, the wooden cottages, and the assortment of trees. Everything looked miniscule yet majestic as the early morning sun rose and stretched its rays across the world below, as if the light was stretching outward from the heavens.

"This must be what God's view is like," Aurora thought in awe. Then she quickly added, "If there is a God."

The adventure continues with
The Change Agent
The Second Book in **The Hypothesis of Giants** series

About the Author

Melissa Kuch first realized her passion for writing after her first story was read before her third grade class. That childhood passion never diminished and instead continued to cultivate with each passing year. Today, Melissa's stories and plays continue to inspire and entertain readers from all walks of life. Melissa's short stories *Cloud Pictures in the Sky*, *To Secure a Husband* and *Name Change* can be found on Amazon.com. *The Assumption* is the first book in **The Hypothesis of Giants** series. Book Two, *The Change Agent*, will be available by 2014. The IDEAL has spoken! For more updates about this series and other works by Melissa Kuch, please visit her website at www.MelissaKuch.com. You can also follow her on Twitter @kuchmelissa

Acknowledgements

Every story is a journey, and this journey would not have been possible without the help and support of so many people. First and foremost, I would like to thank Adam Bock, who inspired me at the Southampton Playwriting Conference to think outside the box and try writing something outside my comfort zone. Little did I know I would embark upon writing this incredible book series. I would also like to thank Maggie Crawford, who edited my first draft and provided such helpful and encouraging advice and feedback to strengthen my work. Her valuable and professional advice helped me realize I was on the right path. I would like to thank Allison Arden for her helpful words of wisdom: once you find something that you are passionate about, everything else falls into place. Thank you to Keri Tan, my amazing photographer, who is a master of the lens and able to capture my personality on camera. Thank you to Ernie Layug and Out-Of-Time Productions for producing and editing my wonderful book trailer. I would like to thank my graphic designer Gerik Goncalves, whose amazing book cover is the perfect depiction of my story in a beautiful and captivating image. I am so grateful to know and to work with such a talented friend. Also, thank you to the wonderful editorial and interior design team at CreateSpace, who worked diligently with me to create this final product that I am so proud of.

I would like to take this time to thank all of my family and friends who have been there for me throughout this journey. With all of your love and support I have strengthened my craft and grown as a writer over these years. I especially want to thank the following people: To my friends Gloria Lee, Laura Ortiz, April Flores, Ellen Lie, Molly Rokasy, Adelyn Ruiz, Billi Vernillo, Michelle Vernaleo, Melissa Martinez, Lauren DeGorter, and Dalila Velez. You have always been there for me, and I thank you for all the moments we have shared, especially when I needed to vent and take a break from writing to hang out with the girls. To my brother-in-law Louie, who has always supported my writing, being my audio tech for my plays and never ceasing to believe in me. To my wonderful sisters Erin and Cassandra, who have supported me since day one and even helped me jot ideas down on a napkin in the early development of this story. They called it the Otus story. I am so blessed to have them in my life. To my amazing parents, my first audience who read everything I ever wrote. They came to my plays and supported me even when they didn't quite get where I was going with this writing thing; but they always told me to follow my heart. Thank you for always believing in me. To my grandma, Eileen Panos; she has a place in my heart forever and I know she would be proud of the writer and woman I have become. Last but not least, I would like to thank my loving husband Mike, who was my first critic and supported me through this entire process. We were fated to find each other, and because of his love and support, this story came to life. I couldn't have done it without him. To all of my readers, I am honored to share my story with you. I leave you with a quote from the musical *Rent*: "There's only us. There's only this. Forget regret or life is yours to miss. No other road, no other way. No day but today."